THAT
GUY
WOLF
DANCING

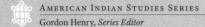
Shedding Skins: Four Sioux Poets
Edited by Adrian C. Louis | 978-0-87013-823-2

Writing Home: Indigenous Narratives of Resistance
Michael D. Wilson | 978-0-87013-818-8

National Monuments
Heid E. Erdrich | 978-0-87013-848-5

The Indian Who Bombed Berlin and Other Stories
Ralph Salisbury | 978-0-87013-847-8

Facing the Future: The Indian Child Welfare Act at 30
Edited by Matthew L. M. Fletcher, Wenona T. Singel, and Kathryn E. Fort | 978-0-87013-860-7

Dragonfly Dance
Denise K. Lajimodiere | 978-0-87013-982-6

Ogimawkwe Mitigwaki (Queen of the Woods)
Simon Pokagon | 978-0-87013-987-1

Plain of Jars and Other Stories
Geary Hobson | 978-0-87013-998-7

Document of Expectations
Devon Abbott Mihesua | 978-1-61186-011-5

Centering Anishinaabeg Studies: Understanding the World through Stories
Edited by Jill Doerfler, Niigaanwewidam James Sinclair, and Heidi Kiiwetinepinesiik Stark | 978-1-61186-067-2

Follow the Blackbirds
Gwen Nell Westerman | 978-1-61186-092-4

Bawaajimo: A Dialect of Dreams in Anishinaabe Language and Literature
Margaret Noodin | 978-1-61186-105-1

Sacred Wilderness
Susan Power | 978-1-61186-111-2

The Murder of Joe White: Ojibwe Leadership and Colonialism in Wisconsin
Erik M. Redix | 978-1-61186-145-7

Masculindians: Conversations about Indigenous Manhood
Edited by Sam McKegney | 978-1-61186-129-7

That Guy Wolf Dancing
Elizabeth Cook-Lynn | 978-1-61186-138-9

*Ottawa Stories from the Springs: anishinaabe dibaadjimowinan wodi gaa binjibaamigak wodi mookodjiwong
e zhinikaadek*
Translated and edited by Howard Webkamigad | 978-1-61186-138-9

THAT GUY WOLF DANCING

A NOVELLA BY ELIZABETH COOK-LYNN

Michigan State University Press | *East Lansing*

♾ The paper used in this publication meets the minimum requirements
of ANSI/NISO Z39.48-1992 (R 1997) (Permanence of Paper).

Michigan State University Press
East Lansing, Michigan 48823-5245

Printed and bound in the United States of America.

20   19   18   17   16   15   14   1   2   3   4   5   6   7   8   9   10

LIBRARY OF CONGRESS CATALOGING-IN-PUBLICATION DATA
Cook-Lynn, Elizabeth.
That guy Wolf Dancing / Elizabeth Cook-Lynn.
pages cm.—(American Indian studies series)
ISBN 978-1-61186-138-9 (pbk. : alk. paper)—ISBN 978-1-60917-423-1 (pdf)—ISBN 978-1-62895-025-0 (epub)—
ISBN 978-1-62896-025-9 (mobi) 1. Indian men—Fiction. 2. Nurses' aides—Fiction. 3. Homicide—Fiction.
4. Indians—Antiquities—Fiction. 5. Whites—Relations with Indians—Fiction. 6. Dakota Indians—Fiction.
7. Indians of North America—Fiction. 8. South Dakota—Fiction. 9. Psychological fiction. I. Title.
PS3553.O5548T47 2014
813'.54—dc23
2013046125

Book design and composition by Charlie Sharp, Sharp Des!gns, Lansing, Michigan
Cover design by Shaun Allshouse, www.shaunallshouse.com
Cover and title page art is *That Guy Wolf Dancing* ©2012 by Ojibway artist Sam English,
from the private collection of C. J. Lynn and is used with permission. All rights reserved.
Interior graphics were derived from *That Guy Wolf Dancing*.

Michigan State University Press is a member of the Green Press Initiative and is committed
to developing and encouraging ecologically responsible publishing practices. For more
information about the Green Press Initiative and the use of recycled paper in book publishing,
please visit *www.greenpressinitiative.org*.

Visit Michigan State University Press at *www.msupress.org*

*This story is dedicated to
those of the indomitable generations who lived vividly
and taught us how to make Art of life's
inevitable companions.*

*History explains neither the natural universe
that existed before it, nor the beauty that is above it.*

—ALBERT CAMUS, *L'été*

THAT
GUY
WOLF
DANCING

CHAPTER 1

I felt a faked intimacy and was reluctant and nervous as I pushed back the curtain to answer her call light.

"Even a li'l smack . . . anything," she agonized.

The woman's smoky voice deepened when I entered her lair, carrying fresh towels from the aide desk.

"Anything . . . anything." She writhed and rubbed her wrinkled hands together and tried to touch me.

I couldn't tell at first glance whether this dark figure was a man or woman. The words spoken weren't spoken harshly, nor was it a demanding voice. It was a voice filled with anguish that left an aftertaste with me that said: *get away . . . get away.*

This white woman, like so many others from around here, was well-off and well-known in the upscale part of this college town located a mere couple of hundred miles from the Crow Creek Indian Reservation where I've been hanging out since I was born . . . just a few hundred miles, but in other ways as distant, like they say, "as the moon."

In this expensive, shiny hospital where I've been working for a while, the doctors are so bored with life and death and money, their wives and children, their pursuits of status and material passions that they just put people away and are not concerned with the implications of how to really care. Unless something puzzling happens. Then they want to know all the answers.

In many ways I understood the callousness of it all. It wasn't a stubbornly held view of myself that I was put on this planet to nurse the sick and the infirm, so my emotional reluctance as a caretaker made me a little anxious and withdrawn. I was here strictly by happenstance, or chance. Some would even call it by accident.

By the time I was getting to know this woman, she weighed less than ninety pounds and was said, by friends in her "set" in a neighborhood isolated from the mere middle class or poor people, to be suffering from "exhaustion." I guess she had been here in this hospital with her wealthy lawyer husband in attendance for years before I got a temp job here, yet she would be in my memory for a long time. Not so much because she was so unique, because she wasn't. She was like a lot of junkies I've known, only she had money and an endowment . . . of sorts.

I can't explain why her awful life, her devastated life, hardly expected or explainable, has been part of the memorabilia about a brief hospital legacy I carry around with me. But, it has. Some things are just unforgettable, etched forever in some kind of personal, yet historical drama.

The room was dark, plush, and seemed to me to be a place for vipers and tree roots and fog and the dead. She was grinning and her face was skeletal and ugly. I was spooked the first time I caught a glimpse of her several days earlier, sitting up in bed smoking a cigarette held in an ivory holder, her eyes shining, her fingers brown and brittle, and I wondered then if a curse had been put on her because she was a princess whose suffocating parents pampered her and left her with no imagination to survive her luxury.

"No, Mrs. Larson," I said as gently as I could, "the nurses say it's not time yet."

Uh-hunh, I wanted to say sarcastically, why do you suppose they sent me, the new guy, the flunky, when your light went on? But there was something about her that made me ashamed of myself, and I hated my rugged response to her terrible needs.

I lifted her wrist and pointed to her thousand-dollar watch and said, "You've got another hour to wait yet, Ma'am." And then I patted her hand and was momentarily horrified when she clung to me and I had to take her hands away from my shoulders and put them beside her on the bed.

"Are you Indian?" she rasped.

She looked at me with terrible eyes, and I walked out of the room, shaken and embarrassed. From then on I did what I could to make her comfortable, but was careful not to let her see that I could be moved by her pain.

I hadn't wanted to end up here, a male nurse aide, all spiffy and white in the longest white uniform Sister Amabolis could find for me after a two-week training session learning how to take temps and empty bedpans and change sheets. And I still don't want to be here, so I never say that I am anything except temporary.

I had wanted to go to Minneapolis and get involved in Indian Affairs when I left the Crow Creek. I even told my Auntie Aurelia that's where I was headed. But then my Uncle Tony Big Pipe shot himself in September of 1981, and right after his funeral I left without telling anyone. From his Dakota tomb he has never said a word to me, and so I have failed to take into account any of the possibilities told to all of us by the whirlwinds of the prairie. And so I'm here. Temporarily.

Now I live in a rundown section of this miserable town. A section made up of mostly old two-story houses that have been here since 1900, fallen porches and cracked paint and old cars and broken sidewalks. But I'm one of those Indians who would never think that just because you live in a dump you have to be a bum, so I never do the drugs or drink the booze I'm offered. I've seen what that stuff can do, and it's not a pretty sight.

When I'm offered pot or LSD or a shot of Early Times to while away the stinking hours in a few moments of forgetfulness, I think of my Uncle Tony, a guy born and raised in a good family, who served his country in Vietnam and shot himself in the mouth one afternoon when the leaves were turning brown and falling from the trees.

Tony had never married and he had no kids. Just me. I lived with him in a little trailer house after I left my grandpa's. We kind of felt like we had each other. Uncle Tony wore his long, silky black hair in two braids and had an archaic longing for total independence and was a man I can now see more clearly than before, a man with a pleasant, quizzical face that promised everything, and a grin that told you how much he loved living. All that makes his suicide even more puzzling.

But most of all, I think of the Valium and heroin shots and Demerol they dish out every four hours on the hour to that young-old woman on the third floor. Nembutal, no one needs to tell me, is what they call yellow jackets out on the streets, and Seconal is redbirds, and codeine is an opiate derivative, and they are on every street corner and in the backroom of every run-down house in any fragile community.

All I need to do when the desperate seller of drugs looks into my eyes is remember holding the ruined white woman over the hospital toilet as she tries to shit or puke or nod off, and remember trying to wake her as she dissolves into her lavish satin bed jacket, unable to turn herself back into a human being even at my insistence.

All this I see every day now.

I know this country, and what I've learned from living with the old gent is that the sacred fire has been nearly quenched, and family scenes for any of us here are not what they used to be. There is nothing piddling about this, nothing even unexpected, since the world changed when they killed off those who knew they came from the land and that trying to understand their relationship to it was their fundamental mission.

Such pain as I see every day was predictable, I guess, in a country now obsessed only with its wealth. The Indian people first understood what the future would hold in this country after the winds established the directions, and later when the four brothers were living alone. They told themselves those stories, but knew they had to bring themselves to accept the demands of wars and kings and power. It was almost like they knew they would be damned, and so would all the others who came here.

It's like the pitiful old-young woman trying so hard to die or to live, an example for all the people whose lives are made up of destructive and obsessive pleasures.

"She hasn't slept all night," complained Robert, the chunky RN from night shift.

"God! Her light on and off. On and off."

He waved his arms.

"You know you don't dare ignore it. Not with her kind of money and private room and long-suffering husband. In fact, he was here until three in the morning putting her light on and off. On and off. Jee-sus!!"

He took a gulp of water from a paper cup, crumpled it, and threw it with great force into the sink.

"Why don't they get a private nurse?"

"'Cuz. No one will stay. They had a private nurse for a while there, but then another one came on and then another one, and finally they just wouldn't do it. Not even for the money, which I understand was way up there."

Robert looked at me hard as though to say we ought to abandon this woman to a destiny without destiny and just let the peace and good will on earth prevail.

The weak will perish and the strong get stronger. Not that I ever thought that was a story of decency.

Robert wasn't a bad-looking guy and he was very smart, but he had little compassion and knew nothing about Indians except what he saw in the movies. He was broad and bulky and white-skinned with a woman's blond fuzz on his freckled arms. He had a full head of curly hair cut short and it made him look boyish, though he was no longer young. Neither manly nor unmanly. The kind of Midwestern specimen whose origins were middle European. Though he had a reputation for being steady and reliable, he was always in a state of agitation, nervous and sweaty, and I just knew from the beginning that we had little or nothing in common.

When I first came to the hospital in this town filled with white folks (there are lots of these lily-white towns in the Dakotas and Minnesota and Iowa) the nuns wanted me to get rid of the earrings in my pierced ears and they wanted me to cut my hair, but I told them no. They wondered what the townspeople would think. I didn't want to reveal any more of myself than was absolutely necessary so I said nothing. Just no.

For some reason, they let me take the job and then helped me get my GED. It took the better part of four months, and all the while I lived pretty much in isolation. I didn't go home and didn't really let anyone know where I was.

While I lived here among them I would be celibate, too, I reasoned, like the nuns and even, maybe, like Robert—though I knew nothing of his personal life—and I would be noncommittal and I would take part in little of the life that was not work. I associated them all with the smell of medicinal pungency and bedpans and the antiseptic cleaning fluids of hospital work.

I didn't allow myself to dislike Robert, but he always patronized me. One time he asked me if I had an Indian name.

"Nope."

I felt like I disappointed him.

And the nuns, well, they sort of acted like they thought I was a well-meaning young man out of place and out of sync with the world but tactful and strong with a reasonably calm bedside manner.

One late afternoon when I came in early for the seven-to-eleven shift, the husband was standing at the foot of her bed, his head hanging and one hand rubbing what was left of the fleshy part of the ball of her foot.

He looked over at me with the sadness of a man filled with an unrelenting grief. "I remember her voice," he said slowly. "No one else remembers her voice, and now look at her. She's just lying there saying nothing."

From where I stood I could see that the hospital did not require underwear, and I felt like a pervert looking in on some strange woman's nudity—someone else's ruined body and someone else's privacy. But the husband seemed unconscious of the ragged display of blackened hips and red bedsores, blue-veined legs, and skinny feet with long colored toenails to match the long colored fingernails.

"Saying nothing," he whispered as though he was talking to her. "Just lying there. Saying nothing."

I wanted to help him. I wanted to tell him to be objective, that she was dying, not living, and that he shouldn't let himself struggle so damn much over the inevitable. Let it go, I wanted to say; sooner or later she would be gone and he had to just let it happen.

I had never known my father, but I always knew he hadn't loved my mother like this man loved this woman. In my family there had been no great gap between peace and ruination, between victory and ambush. My grandmother died of grief, and my mother, while she always claimed she wanted to avoid squandering her legacy as a daughter of an important Indian family, would probably end up senile and disorderly and defenseless and on her knees. What happened to women like my mother was almost as predictable as what would happen to the old-young drug addict whose womanly fortunes and good looks were now spent.

Who knew what kind of woman this old-young woman in this warm private room was. Was she tough and selfish like my mother? Religious? Serious or kind? Needy or independent? Impoverished in this land of maximum luxury? Was it only this devoted husband who knew her voice? I looked at him and knew the perfume of the dying lilacs was the only gift he could give her now, and wondered what he had ever given her before.

I felt bad that this heartbroken man couldn't admit that such an unappealing, humiliated life even at this dying hour was just a matter of human vanity! An incredible waste!

I went home that day, leaving the husband to sit at his wife's bedside, and I was filled with a forlorn sadness, but at the same time glad it wasn't me.

Little did I know, this woman would be a beacon I would pay attention to for a long time in spite of the fact that I've never really known many white folks, having lived in comparative isolation along the Missouri River always. The fact that

I didn't know her well and the fact that I've known the Missouri country forever can be seen as reasons for pondering, however briefly, how they came together.

Anyone interested in the fluvial landscape of the waterways of this country where I've lived, though, has to know that these streams serve as a blank screen, just like my brief encounter with the woman, to provide colorful insights into a nitty-gritty life. Thinking about that poor unfortunate woman, and paying even a little bit of attention to my own love of the life I have had on the Missouri River, gives some clues to how both attractions changed my thinking.

About the Missouri: it has been a continual presence for me and those close to me. Some say there is an underwater being that lives there, too, in the Mni Sosa, and he has a strange relationship with the Dakotah Sioux Indians. Some people understand him better than others. But, for most of us it's just a matter of who you listen to. Some want to hold on to the past, stubbornly and without caring about the harmonious balance which makes life possible.

For me, I just try to get along. I don't think much about the significance of those other water beings, but I know they exist and I believe in them. When I started to work at the hospital I didn't know I'd end up rummaging around in all the things I've tried to ignore.

Sometimes when I wake up in the morning, I'm paralyzed with a sense of catastrophe. Dreams. Dreadful dreams. That's when I need to go home and see people along the river I've known forever. One morning before I had let anybody know where I was, it was like that; and when I opened my burning eyes, a book I was reading fell to the floor with a clunk, and I felt like maybe I'd been underwater, too, like those beings they talk about.

I like to read far into the night, and I tell myself it is maybe not a good thing. Kind of like confession at the altar of the Catholic Church, it's supposed to be good for the soul, but like most recovering Catholics I can't help but be cynical—confessing and confessing, and reading page after page, book after book.

Everybody who knows me knows I'm "fallen away" but that I continue to be an obsessive reader.

I've been reading a lot of "abuse of power" stuff lately. That's what I'm into these days. Politics. Siege and war. Invasions. Migrations. I even started *Jefferson and the Rights of Man*. Phony stuff. Debo's *A History of the Indians of the U.S.* is really more my speed. Mostly because it is such a pathetic story and it seems— more than most—that it is my story.

Reaching for the glass of water at the night stand, I glanced at the clock. Ten to six. The sense of panic subsided. I ought to get up, I think. Maybe I should drive home to visit Kevin. I never did tell him I was leaving.

"You'll go far," he was always telling me. But, hey, I'm not going no place. Crummy job. Never went to the Army, like he did. I'm just barely surviving. Just spend my time reading. Reading. Reading.

As my feet touched the cold, bare floor I felt my bones aching. I looked at the open page at my feet: "*One day the able Mangas Coloradas, chief of the Mimbrenos, made a friendly visit to some gold miners at Palos Altos in southwestern New Mexico. They tied him up and whipped him unmercifully. Understandably, he went on the warpath.*" Page 163, OKLA. PRESS. Debo. 1883.

Eighteen eighty-three. A hundred years ago. It's a nasty story, but my fascination with history keeps books like that on my shelf. I hardly ever read about the tastes and minds of my own generation.

What that means, I suppose, is that the people who are my age really do believe the Sacred Hoop is broken and we all do what we can to survive. Even the chief of the Mimbrenos tried to survive, I tell myself, but what the hell good does it do? He started a war that brought death to thousands of Apaches and devastated a large part of what is now called Arizona. Who survives it? What Indian survives it?

What I call anti-Indian policy, which started a long time ago, is something I think I know something about, but there's nobody around here to talk to.

I looked around the room and found my pants, thrown carelessly across the chair. Slowly, like an old man, I dressed with great effort. My body is a young body, but when I wake up exhausted, lying sleepless in the dark, or reading endless pages of war and intimidation, I hurt all over, damn it! Whatever it is that lives inside of me, plagued by bad dreams, makes it hard for me to get at the chores of living. I brushed my teeth and shaved. Meticulously. Like I do . . . leaving that little bit of mustache the girls like. I managed to do this with cold water, because there's no heat in this house.

The history I read was just hanging out there lingering in my thoughts. No rhyme or reason to it. No stories that seemed very real . . . not like the story I always hoped was in my future.

I headed for Kevin's.

"Where the hell you been?" was his first sleepy question as he sat in the early dawn light already rolling a joint.

When I didn't answer he asked: "What's up?"

"Nuthin'."

The door slammed shut behind me.

Kevin Horse Looking was a man of few words, so the silence hung in the air like the melancholy sadness that filled us both.

"Terrific," he said.

Another long moment.

"That's a heavy sucker"—looking at my book bag I dropped beside the table. "What you hauling that crap around for?"

Horse's attention span was about fifteen minutes. He closed his eyes and leaned against the cupboard. That day he was wearing Bronco orange and blue sweats, grinning without looking at me as I walked in the room to stare at him like I always did, thinking at first glance that his unkemptness was more unkempt than usual. He knew me and he knew what I was thinking, but he was a fan of Christopherson, so he said without apology, "Yeah . . . my cleanest dirty shirt."

That morning, like many other mornings when he shuffled around trying to get organized for the day, he was urging me to quit all the stuff I've been reading, which might, we surmised, lead to college enrollment.

"I'd never tell you what to do," he said while telling me what to do. "You're too smart for me."

He took a long drag on his joint.

"And, I predict . . . you'll go far." He laughed and closed his eyes again as smoke drifted around his face. "Yeah . . . a wolf dancer, hunh?"

I knew what he meant, that I shouldn't try to be something I'm not. We'd been friends ever since we were born, out there in the middle of nowhere along the river, but I also knew that one day he would disappear from my life. He'd be wasted. Never able to manage the physical business of life, let alone the mental or intellectual stuff of living.

He slept a lot, sometimes all day, and I worried about that. In the worst heat of the summer days, he would put on wool shirts and leather gloves and tie his hair in two braids. And, you'd never see him sweat.

He often griped about my running.

"So . . . you do five miles a day. So what?"

"Not every day," I'd say in defense of myself. "Couple of times a week."

"So . . . you think you're going to live forever?"

"Nope," I'd say. "Just until the twenty kids I'm going to have grow up and become something."

He always knew how to control himself. Smile and be cordial.

I started for the kitchen to make coffee.

"There's a lot of outreach these days," I told him. "Outreach for Indian students who want to go to school."

Silence.

I grabbed hold of the aluminum pot, thinking this is the only place I know where they still boil coffee on the stove.

"I could go to Wheaton."

What I'd heard about Wheaton is that they played lacrosse games there way back in the 1870s.

Kevin hardly opened his eyes.

"Fuck," he said.

We somehow got through the morning. I fixed eggs and toast but he hardly ate anything. I went to my car and he followed me out, asking what I was going to do.

"Nuthin' much," I told him.

I drove back to town to sit on the crumbling porch of the old house where I've been staying.

I felt restless.

The sky was gray.

Horse wasn't much interested in my life. Why did I hang around with him? His ragged, red-streaked eyes never really looked at me. He would fix his gaze at the corners of his eyelids and call me wolf.

Somehow, I can't think that Horse Looking and me are telling the whole story. I knew even then I wasn't going to become some kind of academic fuckhead, and I knew he was never going to make it to thirty.

There are some people, no matter how brief their lives, and there are some places, no matter how common, that seem to last forever. Mysteriously, except for the rumors that circulate around us in the little village and rural place called "the fort," nothing seems to happen.

So, the point I make to myself is that it's not sitting in this dump that matters much. It's not my old man I haven't seen for half of my life, it's not even the women I've been to bed with. It's just the place I call home, the river, and I always will need to be there and every now and then make contact with the people I've known all my life. It's that the Grandfathers who are supposed to be your mentors are there, and they tell you about the roads you choose to follow.

Except for my reading and our need to gripe about politics, and Kevin's making fun of how I want to go to college, me and Horse Looking just took care of ordinary matters and didn't worry much about it all.

"Don't sweat the small stuff," he was always saying. And, "You'll go far."

About the roads and the rivers, that's anybody's guess. We call them *wakpalas* out here, and what we know about them is that they've always been wild—lots of currents and eddies and drop-offs—and the old folks always told us that it was dangerous to swim in some of the places we liked.

In the old days the rivers were muddy, full of bullheads and carp, turtles and water snakes. Even now they're mean and they punish. They swell and recede, swell and recede, bringing with them the fertile soil so vital to the prairie lives they embrace.

They are the moving roads of the people and they are the habitat of the spirits known only to the Dakotapi. They sustained the tribes for centuries and eventually brought the fur traders and missionaries into the west.

It's often anybody's guess when the spring rains will come to swell the rivers, but they come and bring with them birds and mammals, and in early May the spring thaw, the ice melt—which is a signal for the geese to leave the ice-free ponds and head for Canada to their breeding places. This is their staying ground where they feed on grasses of all kinds, enjoying the river's bounty. Some of the geese are still there in July, tucking their bills under one wing as though dreading their leave-taking and delaying it even as the heat shimmers.

When we were kids we saw many things along these rivers, but most of all we saw the paths the people made on the ground next to the waterways—roads that were snakelike, winding, useful to whatever vehicles were handy, horses or wagons or cars and buses and even bicycles.

These were the roads of commerce and society, causeways that my mother, Clarissa, called "horse dancing roads." She called them that because she thought she was a great horsewoman and that the roads themselves were almost mythic in the blue fog, like the primordial blue images of *tashunka* that Dakotahs like to think about, an imagined notion of how the previous world meets this one, the journey and the path. That's the way Clarissa talks once in a while. She always surprises me when she talks like that because most of the time she's got no class, no great thoughts, and swears like a trooper. She really never explains the connections . . . horses, rivers, water beings.

By midday the roads often seem circular and rough, hard and loose and unpredictable, heavy with gumbo. These were the kind of roads that kept travelers awake and alert, swampy backwash river roads on the Crow Creek Indian Reservation, makeshift trails along tributaries to the recently channelized Missouri River in a vast country still struggling with change. I grew to know some stuff about these roads as they all led to the natural shadows of a floodlit ground, even though it was easy for a kid to take it all for granted.

Lots of times I walked alone along these roads, or more often, as I rode my horse along these river roads I would watch interloper, long-legged birds. They were like statues, standing immobile for long moments as if listening. They didn't seem to like the dry ground but could be seen standing stark and quiet, heads folded into their arms and their eyes closed, standing ankle deep in warm, brown backwaters, then pecking at unseen things, mossy rocks and insects—first on one leg and then the other for what seemed like hours. Sometimes at dusk I would see them shiver as a way to warm themselves in the evening air.

I had no idea where they came from or what kind of birds they were because I could never find where they nested and there was no evidence they really belonged there. They were *to-ka*, perhaps. I was always curious about them because I saw that their nests, the ones that I could never find, were sometimes placed in the middle of the circle during certain ceremonies that my grandfather arranged.

Who found the nests for ceremony, I would wonder; but when I asked, no one had any answers. My grandfather was a patient man and ordinarily he would answer any questions I put to him, but about the nests he said nothing. I was a curious and meddlesome kid, I suppose, and often asked a lot of questions. Where did these birds come from? Who found the nests? Why were they so hard to find? Could only certain people know where they nested? But, like a lot of things I wondered about during my childhood, I never knew the answers.

As I grew older I asked fewer questions.

Miles from where I'm living now, the old man who raised me to manhood in America is still walking those roads from time to time, and I can see him coming home to roll the new sage into little balls. Tightly he rolls the almost white sage, the male and female sage that grows out in the dry prairies away from the wetlands. Four times he rolls the sage and says in his low voice: *This is a good year for sage.* I can see him in my mind's eye as he places the four balls carefully into the clay ashtray, lights them ceremonially, slowly, and with great longing. He closes his eyes and sits heavily on the narrow, squeaky bed as tiny spirals of smoke rise toward an otherwise vacant, browned ceiling. He draws the spirals toward him and says his prayers.

I am accustomed to seeing this daily ritual in my memory, though now I'm gone from there and now I avoid anything that has to do with religion. I'm what you would call a nonbeliever. I can't say why that is so, because the old gent wants so much for me to believe and I'd like more than anything to please him. It's a hard thing for him to think about the unaccountable changes in the world that have made such a change in me, his favorite grandson. After all, he was born before the turn of the twentieth century, and it's now the autumn of 1982 and he can hardly be expected to care about the idea that this is a year of hypocrisy and dogma like any other in the modern world.

Yeah. It might be *a good year for sage*, as the old man says, but it's not good for much else. The failed movie actor Ronald Reagan has been president for a while now, and the western volcanic mountain called St. Helens out on the coast blew up a couple of years ago. Springsteen is singing a song about America. Stanford University stopped being the "Indians," and Marquette University abandoned its "Willie Wampum" mascot. This is called progress in the modern world, but the old man hardly notices.

It seems to me that no one, not even the old man, is immune to these kinds of events, so I suppose they are worth mentioning if for no other reason than the fact that some people, including me, remember them so vividly. I'm not yet thirty years old, but I know this country well because I've paid attention. I know this country's duplicity and I know how hard it is when you don't control any of the timetables, like my old grandfather who mourns deeply the loss of his family and its place in the world.

Nobody needs to tell me what it means that the old man's eldest son, my Uncle Sheridan, disappeared from the homelands about ten years ago, after the 1973 uprising that took place on the Reserved Homelands of the Oglalas just to the south of us, and we never saw him again, and the federal police kept asking about him, and I grew up thinking he might be just another imagined fool like Tonto or Luke Skywalker. Nobody needs to tell me that all the crimes committed on the Indian reservations of this country, no matter how trivial, become felonious, or that a lethal combination of booze and drugs causes the death of guys I know walking north out of Nebraska toward home. Nobody needs to tell either the old man or me it's a long walk.

This reserved homelands that I come from is a place where my heart breaks. It's like all the places where the presence of terrible truth hits you in the face, where good intentions make you cry, and the dignity of the landscape never fails you. Certain kinds of deficit lives are notorious here in a place like this, and sooner or later, just to find out what's over the hill, you pack your stuff and leave. Not for good or forever, but just to find out what's over the hill.

There's grinding poverty here and ill health, a place so poor that Indian women with children at the knee simply walk down to the water and never make it back, humiliated by the abandonment of seductive and desperate men and insulted by the old, hypocritical ways of the nuns and the church. Abandoned to caring for the next generation with poor health service and no job.

It's been hard to find work around home so that's why I left.

"I don't need no job," is Kevin's way of dealing with it.

But, that's not me. I was always discontent. Looking for something to do. Just hours away there are little prairie towns often filled with people with starkly closed minds, but that's where you can end up scratching a living out of whatever's handy if you aren't careful. I had some idea I'd wind up in one of these what we call "border" towns, but when it happened I was just as surprised as anybody. Maybe that's why I didn't tell anybody I was leaving.

After I sprained my ankle trying to shoot baskets at the community gym the day after my Uncle Tony's funeral, I ended up in the ER of this charity hospital run by Catholic nuns in a little college town not too far away from the rez; it seemed to be one of those places that wants to be of help to those who need it. I just drove myself to the emergency room and they taped my ankle and I told them I was looking for work, kind of on the spur of the moment.

I was pretty much out of line before I got this job, but the people at the hospital didn't know that. I would go to those tribal meetings and rant and rave about all sorts of political things: racism in the schools, the redneck governor of the state and what an idiot he is, how the politicians are stealing the water resources of the Mni Sosa that belong to the future generations, and how the ignorant, self-serving tribal leaders we elect and reelect are doing little about it.

Sometimes Kevin would go with me and he would listen to it all with increasing discomfort.

"Why is it you get so angry?" he would ask, not waiting for an answer which he knew would be long and disconnected. "You're right," I would say. "Why talk about things that happened thirty years ago?"

"But, hey," I would answer myself. "You're no help. You're like a tree of steel. You really don't seem Dakotah. I'm more Dakotah than you are. You just go along and go along."

Accusations like this were just talk. Nothing serious.

Kevin wouldn't smile. He'd just stand there for a long time looking at me. Finally, with a smirk, "Hey, you'll go far."

It's a fact of life on any Indian reservation in the country that native groups and individuals complain incessantly about the federal government, the tribal government, elected officials of all types. These complaints seem to be the major topic of a lot of conversations, even those sometimes with Kevin, and I don't exempt myself from this truth.

One time one of the most well-known tribal leaders of our people went to Washington, D.C., and signed away water rights that belonged to all the tribal nation so that his little band could get back a mere ninety acres of land along the shoreline, I went ballistic.

"That's treaty stuff," I railed at Kevin. "And it belongs to all of us! He's just a councilman and he has no right to sign away . . ."

I wrote letters to the editor of the local news rag, confronted the recalcitrant elected official at tribal gatherings, even participated in some street gatherings. I guess I thought I was pretty smart. Maybe other people did, too, because they encouraged me, but maybe they just wanted to see me make a fool of myself. People who lived down the road from us were always asking me to do things, go to this meeting or that meeting, write proposals. I hardly ever turned anybody down, thinking I was indispensable, I suppose.

I even got into a huge argument with my Auntie Aurelia, who has always been my favorite relative, shouted at her and turned away when she tried to settle me down and told me not to expect reason to prevail in these matters. Justice in Indian Country, she said, "is like flipping a coin." I thought at the time she was giving up, and I was angry. Not angry that she and I disagreed, but that she was just going to say it was okay to do nothing. I wasn't ready then to agree to that, but after Uncle Tony shot himself everything changed for me. Maybe Aurelia's right. Maybe it is just a toss of the coin.

Now that I think back on it, it took a lot of nerve for me to argue with Aurelia in those days since she was just about the only person I could ever confide in and the only person who has been consistent and unwavering in the defense of her life and mine. We're not really blood relatives. She was with my Uncle Jason for a long time and as much a member of the family as any in-law can ever be. When I left it looked like she was getting ready to get married again. The truth is, the thought of her marrying Hermist Gray Bull was another unspoken problem for me. Hermist was a good guy as far as I knew, but I didn't want her to marry him. I didn't want her to get married, period.

On the other hand, I wanted her to be happy. Contradictions. The one thing to say about it is that we will always be close relations, Aurelia and me, even though I hardly ever see her anymore. We will always join our hands in making tobacco ties for ceremony, and our hearts will always be lonely and empty because that's the way we are.

We will always recognize one another's gestures even if we don't know exactly what they mean. One time, long after she left us, she came over to Tony's place where we kept a lot of stuff. She went, kind of in a mechanical way, to the closet, which takes up just the corner of a small room, and she took out a few shirts and found one ribbon shirt that she had made for me and she said, "Is this all that is left of the wardrobe you used to have?"

"Yeah . . . I guess."

She took out a scissors from the kitchen drawer and cut off the sleeves, then she cut out the collar.

"What'cha doing, Auntie?"

She didn't answer, just threw the pieces down, went to the door, opened it, and left without a word.

I watched her drive away and knew she was fed up, not at me but at the way I live, because I always let all of my impoverished relatives and friends come over to our place and take whatever they want or need. Weariness is really the reason she left us, and it may be the same reason I'm here at this hospital carrying around bedpans.

"Hanging out with Kevin will get you nowhere," was the last thing Auntie Aurelia said to me that day, and I haven't talked to her much since then.

Frankly, hanging out at the hospital was no big deal, either.

I was always glad to escape the antiseptic-smelling rooms in this huge regional hospital where this kind of emotional tragedy or others like it were played out on a regular basis. On weekends or when I had a day off I didn't in the beginning go home very often, but I would just fill up my car with gas and go someplace else, anyplace, just to get away.

One Saturday I drove my 1969 Ford Galaxy downtown for parts at Napa. Spark plugs and points would do it. Cost me a few bucks. I walked out of the parts store and lifted the hood and decided I'd do my fixing right there in the empty parking lot. I've made a specialty of keeping this old rig going, not that I'm so good at it. I just have persistence. After I tried to set the points and set the floater there was still a malfunction and I had to take out that little tube in there and clear it out. I'm pretty slow at this so it took the better part of the morning, but nobody bothered me.

I wonder sometimes if it is my destiny to try to fix things, make things that are half shot work again. I went into the store after I finished, found the restroom, and washed my hands.

"Hey," I said to the guy behind the counter as I left, "thanks for the use of your garage."

"Yeah, no problem."

Called "the Limo" by its previous owner, my mother Clarissa, the Galaxy had a rusted-out bottom and a broken trunk latch held down with a bungee cord. Other than being a hard starter and an oil user, the Limo held together pretty good. It was important to me to keep it up, to avoid speeding tickets, and keep it and me out of traffic court.

From there I went to the library to check out my usual weekly stash of books. Sometimes I checked out fiction, but most often I read biography or history; this time I thought I'd try a little fiction about Mexico, *The Good Conscience* by Carlos Fuentes. I'd never been to Mexico and probably never would go there. As it turned out, it was a fairly decent book, a good story, but in the long run it was just a discussion about idealism and the Catholic faith. That's the trouble with Mexico. Catholicism. Every Indian on the continent knows that, but who needs to write books about it? I checked out a "how-to" book on Volkswagens—not that I thought it would help me with the Limo, but it just looked interesting.

With my books beside me, I sat on a bench in front of the post office and watched the people go by. The wind was always a little chilly, but the sun felt warm. Life is good, I was thinking.

The foolish blond girls who passed by had Farrah Fawcett hairdos, and they were laughing, and they carried with them little plastic purses, and I regarded them with contempt and they didn't notice me. No one looked my way. I saw the plump Midwestern parents walk past with their loud, demanding children and I thought: how did these people conquer the world? Suddenly I was lonesome for my Uncle Jason and his horses and his assuring smile. I was even missing Kevin and his smell of mold and bacon grease and *pesi* and . . .

CHAPTER 2

That evening when the sun went down, I strolled around the lighted taverns and restaurants. Anyone seeing me might have thought I was a lonely man, but that would have been a wrong assumption. My great gift is that I feel inconsequential, and my life is satisfactory because it is unregulated and because I know that any real needs I might have cannot be met in this world where I find myself at the moment, so I have no expectations.

It's like marking time, sort of, like when you sit next to the creek and there are quick sounds of the water rushing over the rocks suggesting that it has important business downstream, hurrying, gurgling, but you can just sit there undisturbed, doing nothing. Pleasant. Undemanding.

I glanced at those with white skin, noticed the averted eyes, the perpetual smiles of slightly tipsy women, and listened to the high-pitched sounds of fast talkers. Just people going about their uneventful lives in this strange little corner of the world.

You don't think about death at times like this. No one does. You are just an observer of humanity and you have the mistaken idea that everything just goes around and comes around in some kind of benign inevitability.

So, I was unprepared for what happened when I got back to work the next afternoon.

I don't know why I thought I would probably see the old-young woman again and I would see the husband again and when I did they would be just the same, she grimacing in unimaginable pain, and he attentive, sad, passive. I don't know why I didn't anticipate the fear in him and the danger in the passage of time that led him to be tempted. I don't know why, on this crisp fall day, prelude to the coming snow, I didn't give some thought to what I know best, that the passing of time always changes everything.

Truth is, I just crawled into my bunk bed with no insight about anything except that my knees hurt. I was thinking I wouldn't be around here for much longer.

Next morning at the hospital sink I scrubbed my hands for a long time, still thinking of myself as a transient. I put on my white uniform and watched myself idly in the mirror staring blankly at my impeccable self, a dark man I hardly knew, hair slicked down and a bare trace of the usual grime under my fingernails. At times like these I was just going through the motions and hardly had the inclination to worry about the consequences of what might be happening around me. For me in those days, it was "fake it 'til you make it" time, and though I wasn't self-absorbed, I wasn't paying attention, either.

I passed Robert as I walked out of the washroom into the empty corridor and the whole world changed.

I saw the husband at the door of her room and from the look on his face I wondered if an earthquake had happened, or if all the nuclear-power stations around the world had exploded and we were all meeting our doom. He didn't call out, and the silence of sunshine fell on us through the wide, sparkling windows of the hallway, and I saw him holding the pillow like it was a bayonet or the sacred pipe, and he was looking at me with wild, ragged blue eyes imploring me to understand.

Instantly I knew, and I wanted to say, "I understand. Yeah, man, I really do understand."

But I stood stark still . . . shocked at the calamity of the moment and even more stunned that I'd had no forewarning. I hadn't heard the ticking of the clock and now was helpless in the face of what I knew was an unimaginable brutality. The husband's face seemed to radiate a look of tight-lipped terror, and we both knew almost instinctively that there could never be something so simple here, face to face, as an explanation. As though he hardly knew where the hot liquid that burned his heart was coming from, he sobbed and cried out in an awful whisper, "You're too late."

What are you saying? Too late? Me? No one is alone? No one is alone? On the contrary, we are all alone. Me? Me? I am alone. I don't say this because I like the idea. Not even because I believe it.

The husband glared at me, staring like a madman, and for a moment I felt trapped. Explanations or inquiries were out of the question for me. After several unthinkable, terrible moments I put it away in the same way I had put away the awful bloodletting of my Uncle Tony's suicide months ago. As far as I was concerned, none of this was any of my business.

I turned away from his anguish and walked unsteadily down the long antiseptic hallway to the nurse's station, where I gathered my utensils to take four o'clock temps. I shook so badly I couldn't hold onto the basket of instruments and it fell from my hands, and I spent several moments retrieving the equipment and replacing what was broken. Several nurses, including Robert, stood watching me like I had just gone crazy. Robert bent down to help me.

"Hey, Pipe, what's the matter? You don't look so hot."

"Nothing."

I stumbled out of my near paralysis and went down the hall.

It was a moment of such startling truth that for an instant I heard a voice . . . *deliver us from evil . . . deliver us from evil . . .* like I was at the mission school again and it was the voice of the old priest, and I saw him holding open the book with red-tipped pages, and I heard his voice droning on like exaggerated sheets of rainfall on a hollow roof.

The voice stopped as quickly as it had come, and then there was only silence, and I never saw the old-young woman again, and in the hours that followed, my mind was empty. Meaningless movements I cannot call consciousness seemed to justify my attitude toward this whole criminally vulgar mess and I tried to stand apart from it.

At unguarded and expected times now, though, I think of the husband and that irrevocable moment of terror, which at the same moment is, in my irrational mind, a final act of grace. I will never recite any prayers for him, this tormented killer of his own sleepless woman, but neither will I be his accuser. It's because I have tucked away in the recesses of my brain the notion that life in America just goes down one dead-end street after the other, which means I don't have to make too many discriminations in this environment. Cynics, I read somewhere, never make good moralists, and I had become one of those.

As I saw it then, the husband, like my Uncle Tony, had finally exercised some choice, and perversely, I felt that while this choice seemed most grievous and violent, I wanted to think of it as proper and even admirable and, for sure, inevitable. I decided I wouldn't pass judgment; neither was I going to take any of the responsibility these events and their perpetrators might try to lay on me. As I saw it then, even the sharpest gestures just speak for themselves, but of course I found out in the weeks ahead that not everyone shared my sentiments.

I believed then that there would be no more Days of Obligation for the gentle but tormented husband, none for Uncle Tony, who left me with a smile and touching memories, and none, either, for me, because in the heat of such moments it is often assumed that there is no one to blame. I didn't know then how wrong I was. With the sad confidence of a man incapable of insight, I had thought these things had nothing to do with me.

CHAPTER 3

It was Monday morning following the mercy killing of the old-young woman by her shattered husband that I found myself walking carefully through the visitor's lobby to the elevator trying to be unobtrusive and trying not to pay any attention to the yellow tape the police hung out. It occurred to me that if they were going to call what happened yesterday a police matter . . . a murder . . . I might be first on their list of people to question. When I got to the third floor I noticed a tall middle-aged man in uniform talking quietly with Robert at the desk. Other nurses were standing about, wide-eyed, not saying anything.

I tried to look unconcerned but knew in my heart that these were the kind of people who always seemed to me to be big on sin and punishment and now were probably in the midst of trying to find out every little detail of what happened—a whole truth about a sordid and terrible act that probably should be looked upon as an act of unbelievable courage and compassion rather than something criminal. But, true to the ways of civilized people they would probably negotiate a tedious investigation that would reflect long-moribund values and fragile ideas of right and wrong. I couldn't believe that what the husband did was wrong. Instead I saw it as just one of the saddest things I'd ever witnessed.

I slipped out on the balcony for a quick smoke and looked out on a town that seemed startlingly calm and benign, a place of business and commerce facing itself without much provocation as it had for two hundred years. This is a town that is flat but surrounded by a fluvial landscape of wonderfully sculpted hills. It is easily approachable from the north. It sits along the river, protected by the bluffs which conspire in such rich ways to keep the houses and the people out of the way of the vicious wind that blows off the prairie hills. The stark blue of the sky, the thickets and fields enclosed by wire, tree trunks lying along the slow river current in the summer, and the people walking along the hedges make it seem even more indolent than usual, promising, luxurious.

It's a college town that's been here for over a hundred years, even before a treaty was signed with the Yankton Sioux Indians who possessed the land for, some say, thousands of years. Some say it began as an immigrant place where newcomers from middle Europe could come to grow corn and feed pigs, and it became one of the first college towns in the region even before the Dakota Territory sought statehood in 1889. Indians say it really began as something else, and if anyone cared, its history could make a good morality play, but few people here are tormented by any sticky ethical problems of the white man's recent occupation of the place.

I drew hard on my cigarette and worried that things could get more complicated than I cared for. Because of the way I've been brought up, I'm always a bit paranoid and I was thinking at that moment that things could get dangerous. The white people who settled here knew how to make a system work for them to get what they wanted, power and wealth and a place to live Christian lives. Even though they were rough farmers in the beginning, many of them from the old countries of Europe and others, first generation from the East, they learned how to fake a good society, how to be land speculators and churchgoers at the same time.

They made their own rules about how to live in a righteous way. They started the Dakota Land Company out of St. Paul long before the treaties were even signed, a signal of their self-confidence. DLC was a company that boasted of selling "choice homesteads" out of Indian lands even before they existed. The military generals and captains of the Civil War and Indian Wars settled here in this region and helped make towns like this one to suit themselves. Even the famous Henry Sibley, the hater of Indians and killer of the Santees who had learned to despise the Indian presence very early, got himself elected to the emerging offices of self-government so he could conspire with others to steal Indian land through legislative fraud and the courts. Sibley, in fact, was an officer in the U.S. military who became a model of how to succeed in business . . . the business of killing people and stealing their land. An American hero. Maybe not Kit Carson, but close.

These folks built secondary schools and land-grant institutions funded through the leveling of taxes by their hopeful but inchoate democratic government—institutions where they could train teachers and engineers—and they even started the first medical school here. They built churches, and some even kept private chapels in their homes. They said, "We fear god," but I've never seen much evidence that they really did. Their prayers told them over and over again they were sinners, but seems like they just couldn't help themselves. They loved elegance and beauty. They loved money and power.

What the strict-minded folks of the town didn't love was the wild marijuana that their kids discovered growing along the banks of the Vermillion river that runs through town. It has always been a major crop growing all along the soft, seductive banks. Some say it has grown there forever, but others believe it was brought to this place sometime during the early part of the century when growing industrial hemp seemed like a good idea. Before World War II or just after. Before growing it was made into a serious crime or a silly moral issue that probably has done more harm than good. Would Horse Looking be any better off if he wasn't stoned? To be honest, I don't know.

Whatever the case, this strange and marvelous fact of nature has always made the river a meeting place for the college kids who live in the fraternity and sorority houses on campus. They come here to lie along the banks smoking, trying to get high, and having sex.

Truth is, you couldn't get high on this stuff if you smoked it for a week, but their imaginations and the beer help them believe in it. Afternoons, yellow school buses carrying elementary students home make their way across the highways and bridges, and the younger students look out of the windows of the buses at the remarkable scenes below. They laugh and point as they pass, their faces blurred behind the windows. Often, they turn for a last, staring look as the buses roll on toward the outskirts.

Often in the spring the river crests, and the town which was unaccountably built in the flood plain is threatened. "It's sixteen feet above flood level," the people can be heard to say, the fright clear and loud in their voices.

Or, "My god! It's twenty-two feet above the level." Sandbagging and, later, siphoning water out of dim basements can be read about in the newspapers across the state, and television stories of their courage goes on for weeks.

Clearly no one would think of the traditional ways that Indians had always lived here, moving in and moving out, moving close and moving away in a cycle of nature that showed a real understanding of the river's ways. The same voices heard exclaiming their fears often called these Indians "nomads" and could be heard saying that Indians had never owned the place anyway.

As I looked around for a tray to put out my cigarette, I squinted into the bright sky and noticed that there wasn't a cloud to be seen. I took it as a good sign. I had to pinch the butt of my cigarette with my fingers and scatter the ashes slowly over the ledge, and as I did so I began to realize that there was more to this whole stinking matter of the old-young woman's death than I had first thought. Without attracting anyone's attention, I turned and went immediately to the ward reserved for four old guys and started my cleanup.

None of the old relics looked up as I entered the room. They were lying still, eyes closed and hands folded, as if waiting for their doom. Cheer up, guys, I thought, it's only me . . . not god. Sometimes I thought I recognized my grandfather here in this ward, his spiny legs sticking out of the bedcovers, his soft hands and cavernous voice and the presence of his fleeting grin. But these old Norwegian guys and Germans with bald heads and broken hands looked nothing like him and they seldom smiled. Oddly, they never had any relatives come to visit them.

The floor was slick from recent polishing, and I walked carefully to change the utensils at the bedside of the old guy nearest the door, and he stared up at me with a perplexed look on his face.

"What's the time?"

"It's time for a bath, Mr. Walters." I grabbed the large basin and new towels.

"I don't need no bath."

"Yeah?" I looked around for soap and headed for the bathroom to fill the basin with warm water. He watched me go across the room and, just for the hell of it, decided to argue.

"No. I don't need no bath."

I came back with the pan and drew the curtain around his bed. "You stinky old fart! You need a bath!"

He thought I was funny and started his cackling laugh even as I grabbed his legs and made him sit up, his feet dangling at the side of the bed. I removed his gown and gave him my pretend serious look.

"You probably need a shave, too."

"Nope. I don't need no shave."

We worked together to bathe him, shave him, settle him back in clean sheets, and then he grinned and I went on to the others. Just as I started on the last patient I turned and saw Robert at the door.

"C'mere," he said.

He introduced me to the middle-aged man in uniform. "This is Philip, Sergeant. Phil Big Pipe."

I wiped my hands on a towel and shook hands with him.

"He probably knows more about Mr. and Mrs. Larson than most of us. He was assigned to that wing. Maybe he can tell you something."

The policeman looked me over. He spoke in a loud and firm voice, but there was something uneasy in his manner.

"Well, I know, now, that you prob'ly don't want to get too involved. Most people don't, you know."

He touched his face with his right hand, then rubbed the top of his shoulder. His fingers pulled together his bottom lip in a nervous gesture. I wondered what he meant when he said, "You probably don't want to get involved." I'm not involved, I thought defensively, so why would I care one way or the other?

"How'd the husband treat her?" he asked. "You know, was he okay? Was he understanding? Impatient? Did he care?"

"Sure," I said. "He treated her okay, I guess. As far as I ever saw."

He stood silently and looked at me for a moment. Then he raised his eyebrows and stared away from me, his head nodding slightly.

"Now, look, Philip. We aren't trying to put words in your mouth. But you must know, there is something suspicious about her death."

"No. I don't know."

"They found evidence on the pillow. You know. Saliva. Lip gloss or maybe blood . . . like that. Traces of . . . well, evidence."

"Oh, I don't know." I shifted uncomfortably, shrugged, and said nothing more until he left.

A short time after this I saw Robert in the cafeteria. Seems like he was always hanging 'round.

"You better tell them what you know."

"I don't know anything."

"You'd better get this straight, Pipe. You either tell them what you know or I will."

"What? What?" I gave him a gesture of futility.

"I know you saw him."

"Saw him? Saw him what?"

"You were there in that wing and in that room a lot and I know you saw a lot of stuff. She liked you, and the husband, he was always talking to you. When you were off duty she would ask, 'Where's the Indian? Where's the Indian?' . . . you know . . . she couldn't remember your name half the time but that didn't matter. 'Where's the Indian?' She was always asking for you."

He piled salad noodles in the middle of his plate, pushed his tray down the aisle, and sprinkled bacon bits and beets and chopped eggs in a great heap on the plate. He was agitated and wanted to say more.

Before he could open his mouth again, I said, "Go ahead," half angry at what seemed to be an accusation. "Think what you want. Go ahead . . . why don't you tell 'em? Tell them anything. Make up anything you want. I really don't give a shit. Tell them whatever you want, but Robert"—I stepped closer to him and thought I'd shut him up once and for all—"I don't know anything, Robert. I didn't see anything. I don't know anything. I didn't see anything. You got it?"

He stood still, looking at me, his hands hanging at his sides.

I left my half-filled tray on the counter, turned, and left the room. But if the truth were known, I was worried that I had become an unwilling witness to an impossible and frightful act for which I had no reference, no system, no framework, no philosophy.

The moral smugness of the people who surrounded this unfortunate husband and his awful wife in the face of a seeming selfish and surreptitious act was the only truth I knew. But, surely, I thought, my bare knowledge about the difference between what had happened and what should have happened or what might have happened left me pretty much alone in my thoughts.

After our encounter in the cafeteria, Robert avoided me for a few days. I didn't see the uniformed man again, though others showed up and I heard later that the hospital people tried to make excuses. Even if the husband did do what they might have thought of as the "dirty deed," they rationalized, the woman's death was an inevitable and unavoidable occurrence. It was one of those things that make up the mysteries of life and the mysteries of death at hospitals. Here, in places like this, they reasoned, something that happens every minute in such places like this can't always be known.

Besides, more people die in these places than get well, they said, and she was more dead than alive and had been so for years. So, what's one more? They talked endlessly in small huddles in the hallways, over coffee cups, or in outdoor corners smoking cigarettes, saying this was nothing worth prosecuting and the husband was a victim, poor devil. But the police, with the fervor of moralists they are taught to admire, went on with their relentless, orderly investigation and questioning, and it looked like a huge file of circumstantial evidence was piling up.

The fact that the grieving husband donated money for a lavish wing in the long-care unit helped the people at the hospital and Sister Amabolis and the others forget that what they no doubt considered a crime and a sin had taken place here. Crimes don't always mean punishment, they said in contradistinction to everything they had always said they stood for. And sin doesn't always mean Hell, not even Purgatory. Forgetfulness is a good thing, they said in defense of themselves, and perhaps they should just forget what happened here.

And, finally, there was the suggestion that events based on love instead of malice must be isolated from condemnation, and there was no question in my mind that he did it out of love. Maybe in one of her lucid moments she even asked him to put her out of her misery. No one could know for sure. At the time of private as well as public speculation, I agreed with much of what was said for reasons I don't want to explain even if I could, but even then I wondered why it was that the implication in most tragic events is that everyone is blameless simply because they assume no blame. I knew that included me—for wasn't it up to someone, anyone, maybe even me to have helped this poor guy? Was it okay just to walk on by?

"Where were you when the crime was committed?"

"Crime?"

"You know, the mercy killing."

"Uh . . ." Now it's a mercy killing? Make up your goddamn mind . . . murder? death? Mercy killing? What? What?

"Where were you?"

"I don't remember . . . I don't know . . . for sure . . ."

"Were you there . . . in the hospital?"

"Yeah. I think so. I was on shift, probably."

The police sergeant was tall and good looking and he smelled of aftershave and his heavy dark blue uniform was creased to perfection. The police station was filled with phones and shouts and laughter. The air was heavy with cigarette and cigar smoke and there were no women in sight. A couple of scanners blared.

"We have a witness that places you at the site."

Why was I surprised? Robert, again.

I hunched over my midsection, elbows on the rounded curve of the black chair, hands clasped, and looked him square in the eyes and repeated my answer, "I don't remember."

I don't need this, I thought defiantly. I am the grandson of a Dakotah patriarch, and the revolt of the Santees in 1862 decided my destiny a long time ago. I am not obligated like the people of the middle class of America to answer to the police even though they've been on every reservation in the country like fleas on a dog's back since 1840. And here they are now, in places where they think they have jurisdiction, bugging people, harassing. What's the point?

"We're not trying to indict you, Mr. Big Pipe," he said with what I saw as his own pretentiousness.

"We know you had nothing to do with it. So, you don't need to be afraid that you will give evidence on yourself that will get you into trouble. We are just trying to establish witnesses to a crime."

"Uh-hunh."

"Now we are truly honored that you have come in at our request. We are pleased that you are going to be of some help."

I hunched down in silence.

These people who have now become the caretakers of law and order in this part of the country were alien to my thinking, and I simply had not ever had much to do with them. I folded my arms and wondered about the past and how these people got here; the land laws of the Yankton Treaty didn't give them the right to this place. They had no right to take over and plant crops and feed hogs and harvest alfalfa and wheat and corn like nobody lived here, like this was some kind of vacant place. The whole countryside stinks because of their doings and now they're questioning me. And, just for the hell of it I'm not going to tell them anything! Defiance is a strange thing. It comes out of nowhere when you least expect it.

"We need to know what happened."

Why can't they leave the poor devil alone? I thought. This kind of haggling and verbal aggression filled me with disgust and I said nothing. But, he wouldn't give up.

"Now, Mr. Big Pipe. Can you tell me what you saw?" Over a white desk pad he held a pen in his large, broad hand.

"I didn't see anything."

"Did you see Mr. Hanson come out of the hospital room where his wife was?"

"Nope. I don't remember nothing. I saw nothing."

In the interrogation room I had been seated next to a tall, very thin white boy with big, trembling hands that he used to gesture when he spoke. His back was turned away from me and I could not see into his eyes, and I wondered what strange and improbable events had brought this poor sucker into the presence of these assholes. As I walked away I saw his pinched face, his red nose. I felt desolate as I heard his quiet weeping.

CHAPTER 4

By the following evening I had pretty much forgotten about all this interrogation, which seemed like a bunch of crap to me, when my mother showed up driving a pretty decent-looking Chevy pickup. New tires and an intact paint job. Gun racks in the back window held a .30-.30 rifle and a .410 shotgun. It was about seven o'clock.

It was always the same when I saw my mother, Clarissa. Uncertainty. Denial. Dread. I hadn't made a practice of going home to her house to visit, so she always had to come looking for me, which was a puzzling phenomenon because I knew she didn't really care a thing about me. Not like Auntie Aurelia, who helped raise me or at least taught me much of the stuff I needed to know to survive in a world where most people want you to be "all you can be" just like the Army says.

I hadn't lived with Clarissa for years, and besides, I was always too radical a thinker and I always read too much to get along and be accepted in the places where I grew up. My mother hated my reading. I guess I was one of those people who knew the writings of too many authors and scholars, knew the history of the people, and was taught by the old man what was really dangerous, not merely annoying, in this world. I always knew more history than the nuns and the priests who taught at the mission—"cloistered" wasn't just an adjective to these people, it was a way of life. So, when I got fed up with school during Holy Week the year I was sixteen, I made a couple of decisions. I sang in the boy's Latin choir at Stephen Mission for the last time, took communion with my mother after having refused confession, and decided I'd had enough of my mission schooling.

I hung around the rez for a few years not doing anything. How I ended up here is anybody's guess. Some guys, all they want to do is fool around with women or play six-string guitar with Robert Earl King on Austin City Limits southeast of Dallas. Or maybe with Lyle Lovett, a guy who's got the best western band outside of Nashville and hair that looks like it belongs to a scared porcupine.

But me? I just want to be who I am; I want to be an Indian living on the homelands of the people. That's all. Trouble is, I couldn't get much of an education there except to read the lives of the saints in the assignments they gave you in religion classes, or the white fantasy life called *Little House on the Prairie*, where there are no Indians in what we all know is Indian Country. But more to the point, I couldn't find a job there, and so after a while of doing not much of anything, and after my Uncle Tony shot himself, I left. An economic exile, you might say. And an exile from having to think about the real or the unreal, the foolish Western fantasies about friendly Indians, or the bloody death of a man who meant more to me than most fathers mean to their kids.

What I'm doing now is not much, either, but maybe it's better than throwing bales for room and board from some white farmer who leases Indian land for pennies. This river town with its state college and this hospital nurse-aide job . . . it's the pits. I'm not ever going to get used to washing people's body parts, lifting the helpless when they can't lift themselves, and emptying their bedpans. When I put it that way and really think about it, maybe it's not better than throwing bales.

The evening Clarissa came into the restaurant where I was eating my never varying supper, a hamburger and fries and a Coke, I was kind of surprised because I hadn't seen her in a while. Her gaudy scarf tied around her neck, her majestic tribal face appearing out of nowhere. I looked at her steadily for a minute before I turned back to my supper, both if us with closed expressions like we had secrets we didn't want to talk about.

"Why'n'cha order me a beer?" she asked as she sat down across from me, "or is this place too fancy for beer?" She took off her gloves and shrugged out of her light jacket. Rubbing her hands together, she looked around, and I knew she was either in the process of tying one on or she was just in one of her snotty moods.

I didn't say anything.

"Are you still working?"

"Uh hunh." I waved to the waitress. "You want something to eat?"

"No."

"Miller Lite," I said to the waitress.

"Sorry," the waitress said. "Millers don't make no light."

"Yeah, they do."

"No, they don't."

"Well, how about Grainbelt?"

"They don't have no light, neither."

Well, I thought, why argue with such a moron. "Grainbelt, anyway."

"Yes, sir." She swept up my dollar bills.

We, Clarissa and me, we belonged to a well-known family, one that had a grand old man as patriarch, well thought of, literate. A real Dakotah. He was lucky in many ways, had four sons and three daughters, one of whom, Clarissa, was my mother. By the time I came to know his life, though, and his children's lives, they were middle-aged and the old man was broken, and his wife, a grandmother I barely knew, had gone to the other world.

These parents had spoiled my mother, their middle daughter, as they raised her. I don't know why except that she was said to be exceptionally strong-willed. They let her be selfish and frivolous and insolent until she fooled around with one loser too many and ended up having two kids, a boy and a girl, as a single parent, then married my father, who was from Pine Ridge, and bore my brother and me. She soon kicked him out before I could walk or talk and then told everybody he had abandoned us, and since then I have known very little about him.

It is always difficult for the children of old families. Since my mother was a daughter of the Big Pipe *tiospaye* it was expected that she would have a good life. But by the time she came along, much of the life by which the family held prestige was gone. When she was a young woman, there was much change and land loss on Indian homelands in the north country and there were many contradictions. About the only way people had of "making it" on the reservation was to work for the Bureau, the U.S. and/or tribal government, or the churches, and since Big Pipe would do none of the above, there was considerable uncertainty in our family.

It's not that my mother had any pretensions about all that. It was just that there was no place for people like her anymore, women who just wanted to have a family and make dried deer-meat delicacies and have lots of dogs and horses and feed everybody. Big Pipe had tried to make a world in haying and ranching and horses for his sons, but in the modern world that meant there wasn't much of a place for his daughters. Clarissa had little education and no job and lived mostly off the charity of her family. We were often on welfare.

"He was mean and a woman hater and he drank too much," Clarissa told us about my father. "One time when he came home drunk he chased me down the road in my bare feet and pajamas in the middle of winter and I had to hide out in an old shed until morning. Nearly froze to death."

That was the extent of my learning about my father's behavior and why I never grew up with him, but the truth is I never put too much faith in her stories. I don't hold grudges.

It seems odd to say I never missed him because everything you hear and read today tells how terrible it is to be fatherless. One of the reasons his absence didn't matter, I suppose, was that everything in those early days centered around my grandparents, and I had uncles and cousins and a community of males and it didn't seem like I was a fatherless child. I just never thought about it. There was always a broad show of affection toward children and an understanding that children were the wealth and the future.

"You know why I'm here?" my mother asked.

"Nope."

"Because your grampa is very sick. I think he is dying."

She took a long slug of beer, which she drank from the bottle even though the waitress had brought a glass.

"We're all dying, Clarissa," I said with some degree of certainty as well as despair. "He's been sick a long time. He's just old."

"Get your things together and come home," she said, pursing her lips and tasting. Full of directive. As though it was settled. Maybe her directive was an act of impossible fate, I thought as I watched her fidget, wiping the cold sweat from the bottle. Unavoidable in the grand scheme of the life of a mother and her son.

Get your things together and come home, she said, as though one could look out on this world without surprise and without consequence. It was all very simple to her and yet so very complicated as far as I was concerned. I guess I could go about becoming the kind of man who does all the things he's never wanted to do, I thought. Always the opposite of what he really wants to do.

I don't want to be a nurse aide in this ridiculous town, but I don't want to go home either. If I went home right now I would have to think about the horrible death of my Uncle Tony, maybe even live in his trailer house where the last time

I saw him he was on the floor in a pool of his own blood and Clarissa was holding him and crying about her own grief and he was limp as a dishrag.

I might have to face the awful unspoken truth about Clarissa, that she is a selfish, self-centered woman who never really gave a shit about anybody but herself, and never gave a shit about me except when I could do what she wanted, fetch her cigarettes or do the dishes.

There was something uneasy about our mother/son relationship even at the beginning. No one knew that she often said to me, "You're just like your father." No one needed to know that she beat the hell out of me when I wouldn't go to school or when I resentfully blew out the candles she would light in the evenings for her hypocritical prayers. What people did know, and what her parents talked to her about endlessly, was that she would leave us at home, alone, for days on end and would come back hung over and shrill and mean. Her parents and everyone else knew that she was the perfect and willing companion for the drunks she so despised.

If I went home now, I might even have to think about what happened to my father and my disappeared Uncle Sheridan, though no one ever talked of these matters. Not ever! No one ever talked about these matters, and it is always the unspoken things that are responded to in memory. Holding onto the family traditions, we were taught to show little affection, avoid quarrels, avoid gossiping and criticizing one another, and try to remember that you were the grandson of old so-and-so, or the ideal wife of someone, or the head of a good family, or a member of this *tiospaye* or that one.

Whenever somebody asked you, "*Taku iniciapi he?*" that was what he was asking about. Being a good relative was always at the back of these traditions. But, these were nothing but transformations of the imagination—ideations, they're called by the literate folks—rather than real life, and we all knew it.

If I went home now, as Clarissa was demanding, I would have to think about the coming death of the old man. Maybe one of the reasons I left so suddenly in the first place was because I didn't want to have to think about that eventuality, the most dreaded of all expectations. Sometimes when I look past the dullness of my present life, beyond the certain wisdom of matching questions to answers, or answers to questions, I get to thinking about how things are changing. So fast.

Some guys I know start thinking that if there is a god, he sure as hell fails to look down and see us, and they start thinking, instead, that in the face of such indifference, maybe they need a drink before they go home to their empty lives and empty rooms—but that's not for me. For sure, I am depressed about how things aren't like they used to be, or like they're supposed to be, and how every day I have to look out for obstacles in a road that seems to be going nowhere, and how self-righteous and logical the people I work with seem to be.

Yet, I manage to continue to believe that the steps one takes in this life are governed partly by the state of one's health, one's mood, and the demands of one's daily duties. You know, just one day at a time.

I looked across the booth at Clarissa and noticed how old she had gotten since the last time I saw her, which wasn't but a few weeks. She seemed much smaller than I remembered, shrunken, and I didn't know if it was because of the cold air of the evening or if she was just shriveling up in her old age.

Another tooth was missing from her bottom jaw and her once regal bearing now just seemed permeated by physical weakness. For some reason I thought about how vital she had once been, how she rode horses and drove cattle for her dad even in the dead of winter. She was a strong rider. Aurelia was, too. These were women you could say really knew horses.

"She doesn't miss a thing," her dad used to say about Clarissa, and I never knew if that was a good thing or a bad thing. She wore cowboy boots every day of her life, shined to perfection, and jeans, and she was always reminding me when I was a kid to "look good." In those days she cared about her appearance. In the winter she wore a yellow "slicker" raincoat over her parka, and it was nothing for her to ride into the snow-swept hills to help find a critter or drive cattle away from the river. I always felt she didn't get enough credit for the work she did around the place. It was always her brothers people depended on.

I remember the old cow dog Clarissa kept. He never had a name. She just called him "Dog," when she called him at all. I remember the heaviness of that old dog's limbs when he could no longer jump into the bed of her pickup, and I can see her, like everybody else, giving him a boost. Or that horse she used to ride, that bay mare that got so old, one winter day she just went down in the corral and never got up. Froze solid in the icy manure and had to be hauled out in the spring. Even the animals around the old man's place and at Clarissa's are no longer what they once were.

Now Clarissa's dark hair is streaked with gray. I noticed her careless appearance, her worn jacket, and while I wanted her to go away and leave me alone, at the same time I felt sorry and somehow responsible.

I took a deep breath. "I've wanted to do things," I said, as a way of avoiding her directive.

"What things?"

"Oh, I don't know."

She looked at me with anger in her eyes, like I might have been my father on that icy occasion when he chased her down the road. Anger is a made thing, I thought; it's not just an inspiration. It's a way of being in the world, and I recognized the loneliness that was at the bottom of it for Clarissa.

"I don't understand you," she said accusingly. She was on a roll now and would give the guilt-tripping all she had. "You leave and don't even tell nobody where you are . . . where you're going . . ."

Talking nonstop, she signaled the waitress for another beer.

"And you're gone and nobody knows where you are. I had a hell of a time finding you, had to run around the reservation asking anybody if they'd seen you."

I said nothing. I pulled out my pack of cigarettes, offered her one, and we lit up.

"What are you doing here?" she gestured, trails of smoke coming out of her nose and mouth. "You wanna be a hospital nursemaid all your life?"

"No."

"Well, what then?"

"Well, I just came here. Sort of by accident."

She stared disgustedly, wrinkled her forehead, and took another deep drag from her cigarette.

"Accident?" Her voice was almost a sneer.

"I was going to go to Minneapolis but then I didn't."

After a pause I said tentatively, "I thought about law school."

"Law school?" She nearly screeched.

It had occurred to me, though I didn't say anything to Clarissa, that I probably couldn't even get into law school, let alone become a lawyer. I had a felony against me for selling eagle feathers. These aren't just minor crimes and misdemeanors to the people around here, and to this day I am ashamed to say I wasn't able to pay off the fines and had to lay it out in jail.

I always felt that my mother didn't believe in kindness as a principle, nor did she want to believe that her kids had a right to their own lives. My older half-sister, Rosie, still lives at home and is a virtual slave to our mother's bossy ways. It is a sad situation there. Rosie does nothing much around the house, very little for herself, and mostly sits around and watches TV, afraid to leave and even more afraid to confront Clarissa, who believes in telling other people what to do.

I wonder sometimes if the failure of my mother to let my sister become an independent woman, the failure to put on a "feed" and declare the appearance of womanhood for her daughter, was because it was never done for her.

What I've noticed about us nowadays is that we often can't bring ourselves to acknowledge that those old manners could still be important to us. The Santees used to have a big feed when a girl became a woman and was looking around for a husband so she could have a life of her own. They would cook berries mixed with fat, and the prayers in the community often said grand things like *wi-ca-sta ya-ta-pi wo-yu-te de-ya-tin-kte*—which was an invitation to eat the important food, the chief's food, the father's food, or in some cases the grandfather's food, prepared on a great occasion by the family. Food has always been a big deal and they like to have big feasts. They always cooked too much so that the people would have to take it home with them. They had a word for that in our traditional language, *wa-te-ca*; sometimes they say *wa-te-hi-ka*, and it is translated something like "that which is dear to them." You give away what is dear to you. That's a big deal, too, a principle of how to live a good life.

I've never known what all of this has meant, and I don't know exactly what those prayers meant, but I think they were important to families and in the old days they helped young people to move toward independence. Now there is not much of that going on, and the truth is, even if it could happen in our family by some miracle of everybody pulling together, I don't see Clarissa helping out much. I knew as I looked at her that our attempt to communicate this time would go from bad to worse, turning into its usual disaster. I took a huge bite out of my hamburger and stuffed my mouth with fries. I saw her look at me out of the corners of her eyes and noticed her upper lip and thought, "So this is what they call a stiff upper lip, hunh?" Nope; swallowing a huge chunk of hamburger, I knew then that this woman who is a mother to me just holds me in great contempt, and the truth is, I no longer had the need to wonder why.

CHAPTER 5

It's true the roads traveled have been roads to uncertainty and disappointment, but we've never given up hope that the ancient, beautiful, indolent, expansive country of our ancestors might become what we need to survive.

After my supper with Clarissa, I stood on the empty street, my eyes filling with unaccountable tears. I lit another cigarette and took several long, hard drags, blowing the smoke toward the chilly darkness. There was no wind. Every now and then the headlights of a car appeared around the corner.

I don't ever remember how my personal standoff with my mother began, but it had something to do with what I was listening to in this silence, a longing for the wind in the trees, the smell of the river.

To get to the old man's place from here you take I-90 for about three hours and turn off at a little river town called Chamberlain, a muzzled and tight community of people of European immigrant stock who have always hated Indians. A border town, home to the Chicago and Northwestern railway traffic of the old days. Also a place where Indians, women and children and old men, hid out along the banks of the river during the times when U.S. Cavalry troops scanned the water and landscapes with killing in mind.

It was on this turnoff road that my Great-uncle Lawrence, the old man's brother, walking back to the rez after a two-week drunk, was downed by hit-and-run, and when the police investigated, they called it an "accident." Here on this road when I was a kid we used to stop the car so my mother's drinking boyfriend, whoever it happened to be at the time, could get out and sit on the shoulder of the road and puke, and then he'd get back in the car and moan and cuss. Like all thoroughfares, this little turn-off road to the reservation holds the secrets of an entire generation.

You look at those fluvial hills along the Missouri and just follow them north. When you drive at night you can look at the sky, and if it's clear, if there's no fog rising from the water, you can see what the white men call the Big Dipper; we call it something else, but it's the seven carriers of the people and carriers of all the good things in this life. On such clear nights you can see the shining seven stars that make up the constellation called *wica akiyu hanpi*, and you can see the bear's home in the sky and know that there are ancient customs referring to the moral beings held aloft in the stars, customs that are still practiced by people who care about these things.

For me, I'm like a lot of people I know who seldom do religious rituals or ceremonies and then complain that nobody does those things anymore. But once in a while, in the silence of the stars, whenever it happens to be the right moment, I take it as a privilege to just stand there and stare into the heavens because it seems more than likely that we are, like the old man says, related to the stars as Dakotapi. It's rare times like these brief encounters that I think maybe I'm a believer after all.

I've lived there along the Missouri for most of my life, and that's where I got to know the world and that not all people are the same, just like not all rivers are alike. That's where I got to know Aurelia, my favorite relative-in-law; that's where I decided to reject any of the religious beliefs I'd been taught in school, although to please the old people I sometimes follow public rituals as a way of acknowledging the possibility that they could be right. I still do that when I'm faced with some things the old people care about, and it may be accounted for as the price I pay for my independence from self-examination and self-inquiry.

I learned from Aurelia, though, that most religious rituals are not really a way of knowing something. They are, instead, just a way to remember what you already know. Aurelia is one of those people who believes that the meaning of life represented in physical geography is the only thing that should interest us. And rituals that people do are only useful if they connect the people to certain holy places. She used to say that what the spirit people do and where they bring certain things to the people as gifts are the places that are considered sacred.

I never was able to talk about these things, these philosophical things until she taught me, and even then it has been very hard for me. It is almost a different language that she would use and it allows her to say nothing is "for sure." Still, the things she admires in life, mysteriously, helped me to understand that there are ways to defend yourself against the encroachment of others.

Since then I've understood there are some people who just simply don't fit the stereotypes. People like Aurelia. People like myself. You know, the stereotype of Indians being losers, or stoic, or whatever. You know, vanishing and all that, shot out of the saddle by John Wayne. You've got to have confidence. And since I've come to understand that ties to specific places on our homelands mean everything, I've tried to have confidence that someday I may come to rely on them. If not now, someday.

Home is that place where they have to take you in if or when you come. Anytime. Under any circumstances. Knowing this is part of what gives me the courage to do things that aren't ordinarily expected. I don't mean the home Clarissa made for us. I mean the home the old man has always kept; but the truth is I've never made my peace with what goes on at home. One time a long time ago, I sat on the porch with the old man in the late afternoon. It was just after we had gone over to Guy St. John's place to help him build a little porch onto the back door of his house just off the kitchen, and we were exhausted. It was hot and the sun was going down and everybody was heading home. As I watched the dust clouds rise behind somebody's speeding Ford van going down the road, I felt detached, like I was watching a specter, an unreal thing in the haze off the river. Beyond the rolling hills, I said to myself, there is something real over there beyond the hills and beyond the river, and someday I want to find out what it is.

No one knew of my feelings at that time and I couldn't express my feelings to my grandfather, but I was aware of the odd gaze the old man gave me when I greeted him, so he probably knew even then I was restless. Maybe my mother Clarissa didn't keep the little beaded water-animal fetish with my dried umbilical cord in it attached to my cradleboard long enough. What do they call that? *Che-k-pa*? Something like that. Keeping it is a custom of Dakotah mothers who always want to keep their children near and even have private words to express their emotions when their children are absent from them. *Wahdechapi*. It's a woman's word. Maybe I was one of those that left the cradleboard too soon.

Now, much later on an autumn day standing on the banks of the river near his place, the old man listened to me as I told him that Clarissa wanted me to come home for good. He didn't say anything right away, and then finally said in his absent voice, "You must pay close attention to what surrounds us." I wondered if he had heard what I'd said, so I said it again that I wasn't ready to come home just yet, and assuming nothing, his face a pleasant mask, he said that was fine. Jason stood with us and he said, too, that it was all right for me to do what I wanted, that I didn't need to worry about anything, that he was there to take care of the old gent.

We got our tools out of the car and stood there mesmerized by the late afternoon sun high in the light sky. "Just because we were once the star people," the old man said, remembering what was important about his life, and wanting to help me forget about the claims Clarissa was always making, a dissatisfied woman who always wanted things done right now, a woman always in a big hurry, ". . . just because we were once the star people . . . that doesn't mean that we don't belong to the earth.

"In those times . . . when we were *oyate wichacpi* we journeyed into the real world by the sky path. Just because that is so, though, that doesn't mean we believe in heaven. We don't believe in heaven, not in the way the *wasichus* do, like it is the home of god or the angels, not even that it is a place of extreme happiness. The sky path is just a path to humanity and it can only be understood if we know that water is its source, if we remember that the earth and the sun forever have a sensitivity to one another." He said all this in Indian and it doesn't sound so formal in that language. It's just the way he talks.

The old man told another story that other time, that long-ago time when we were again standing next to the river. It's funny how I remember all of these things. But then, this one was a repetitious story, not one that was connected to the old ways, a present day story that I've heard many times, told again and again as a recent happening; it's one of those tellings that indicated how much it disturbed the people.

He said that a couple of years ago, maybe in 1980—though he couldn't remember the date for sure—this was the place where American Indian remains and artifacts were found, and they became the subject of much controversy. He remembered that museum people and college professors came to record their findings, but they didn't ever tell the people what they found out. As Grandpa talked slowly in his hollow yet sensual voice, Jason and I lifted our eyes to the darkened river, and a damp mist seemed to lower itself to surround us. The distant cottonwoods silhouetted in the dusk muffled the sounds of a loon or a bird of some kind noting its presence in the distance. Again and again.

"Thirty years after the U.S. Army Corps of Engineers was supposed to have moved a cemetery for the construction of the dams," the old man said, not finishing his sentence. "Thirty years . . ."

Low water levels and erosion could have caused the uncovering of these remains, but the real question asked in the mist that night was the old man's question: if the Corps moved the cemetery thirty years ago, as they said they did, why then were these bones strewn at the water's edge?

Why, after thirty years, after hundreds of graves were supposed to have been moved, did we see remains exposed with fabric material and artifacts supposedly buried forever with the dead? So the other question was, are these really thirty-year-old bones or are they three-thousand-year-old bones or are they three million years old? Whose are they? Whose relatives are here? Only the loon spoke to these questions in the distance and I stood still in the eerie light. Deep and haunting sounds filled the air.

Finally, the old man interrupted the sounds. "These souls were not kept and have not been ceremonialized in the appropriate way. This is very dangerous."

Grandpa—or so it seemed to me then—was getting just like another old man who was his predecessor, Grey Iron, a man who died when I was very young, a man I don't really remember, can't even recall his face. But I remember his funeral and I remember he was a man whose funeral was like a *wacipi tashunka*, a horse dance. I remember his death because of the many horses they had in the cortege and how grand they looked in the broad daylight. It wasn't a sad funeral like one would expect. At least I didn't see it that way. It was in the morning and the sun was shining. Really bright.

I was just a kid then and I had a great imagination. I imagined it to be like a triumphal approach to the sun, and the spirited horses, some with riders and others without, pranced and danced for two or three miles all the way to the burial ground. I sat on the front fender of a cousin's car and watched it all, and it has become one of the memorable images of my childhood.

Inescapable times those were. When I think back on those times, I wonder if we are supposed to believe that all of life is a dance, like that dance of the horses I witnessed as they were leading the spirit of the old man to another world. I'd like to think that. In my heart I know the steps you take lead nowhere unless you attempt to direct and control and develop the dance itself. It's an understatement to say that I'm not into it, but if you don't try to demand something of yourself and be attentive to the dance in whatever forms it presents itself, memory or reality, it simply becomes a dance on a road that leads nowhere. Maybe that's where I am now. I know all these things, but somehow I consider acting upon them an intrusion and I continue to resist. People think I'm just an Indian guy without much insight, just "doing my thing," sort of, but the truth is, I'm a Santee Dakotah born and bred, which means it is my obligation to be something more than a guy just occupying space.

I wonder about these things and worry that I will never really get it. It's just that I'm afraid I can't . . . I don't know . . . it's just that I'm never in the mood to make a commitment to it, apparently. So, what does it matter? Well, for sure what I've learned over the years is that the dance is only memorable if the dancer has control of the gestures of it, and if he is graceful, and if he doesn't step on the others and push them.

My mother was there the day of Grey Iron's funeral, as she often was when the ritualization of events took place. In truth, she always put forward a good face. Her face on that day was the plain and passive look of a woman who has exercised few good and useful choices in her life, a woman who has little or no dancing skill, but even she seemed to be consoled by the horse dance and the cortege we were witnessing.

"Look at the horse dancing," she said. "Remember it, Philip." In the face of such good advice, it was hard for me to remember her vulgarity, her pretenses, her playing a part on her stage of motherhood. Together that day we had listened to the talks given by those who were doing the right thing.

What they said about the old man they were burying was that he was forever reciting history, humanizing the past, telling the people that something huge and terrible had happened in our long history in this country. And the people would wonder, was it myth? was it real? Being around these old men and their rituals was like being around an indefinable yet powerful atmosphere, but I always felt there was something I missed. I would get the feeling that I was left out, and it often brought about a strange preference for turning away, a hollowness that wouldn't leave me. In some awful contradiction, I longed for the time when men like him could not read.

Zuzuecha rises above Medicine Creek, in the forgotten words of the old man, *right there in what eventually became Hughes County. North of the Crow Creek Indian Reservation and a little west.* He said: *The people put rocks angling off to the north, in the form of a huge snake so they could commemorate those times of becoming, those times when the world was just beginning. It was a kind of memory device.* He told them: *And it was along the length of twenty or more tipi rings, undulating and perfect, wide in some places and narrow in other places, and the stones comprising the outline of the tail were much smaller than those used for the body, no larger than a fist. The turtle and the waterbug are nearby on a bluff, on a kind of summit that rises from the land. The people loved this place and they camped there where their horses danced in the sun and bore many foals. We are never to be robbed of this reality,* old Grey Iron had told them, and they stood in silence even then.

I never heard these actual words and stories of the elders, so it is only at times of grief that I feel this awful loneliness. Then it is that people remember and talk and we are reminded that speech is sometimes useful, and sometimes silence is even more useful for understanding that a huge history has made us who we are and that the final act has not, yet, been played out.

Remembering Grey Iron and what they have always said about him, and thinking about Clarissa, I stood beside my grandfather and watched the yellow jackets swarm sluggishly and chaotically, kind of a slow motion, in the nooks and crannies of the river debris and knew, as they did, that it would soon be the end of such dizzying times.

I have listened to all kinds of stories, but my grandfather's story on that day along the river was solemn and believable, not just something from long ago. I lit a cigarette and, drawing the smoke deep into my lungs, I closed my eyes just for a moment and forgot about the yellow jackets, the ceremony for the dead, and the horse dancing. I forgot about the antiseptic smells of the hospital and about the sad old-young woman, and I forgot about the old guys in the ward who never had any relatives visit them. I smoked in silence for a few moments and then threw down my cigarette and ground it under my foot.

Forgetting that Clarissa wanted to run my life, I stood there thinking I would like to see the river and the sun somehow work together to erase the centuries of man's struggle to distinguish himself, so I wouldn't be burdened about making decisions. The river looked cold, but it was so rich and filled with the look of the soft earth that without thinking I stooped down, took a handful of dark sand, and threw it over my shoulder with my right hand, another handful over my left. I needed some good luck, I thought. Something. Some sign.

The sky was turning gray and then blue and then lighter and lighter, and eventually the orange of the sunset was so bright. It reminded me of when I was a kid at the peyote meetings and I was warm in the blankets on the hard earth and, nearly asleep, I would watch the colors become so bright in the darkness and listen to the sounds made by the people and the water drum. Its seven stones would hold the songs, which would become almost garish and hard to listen to, and I would feel like I wanted to get away. I was just a kid, but I knew even then that watching the days and nights go by without finding some direction is prelude to nothing, not adventure, not understanding. Nothing.

Standing in the presence of the old man and my uncle, the fresh smell of the autumn wind trailing along the shoreline made me think of how I would like to flex my own muscles. I spit on my palms and took the ax and began to chop some firewood, and it felt good to hear the piece of iron strike the wood. As I worked I came to the conclusion that I could make up my own mind about when I would be coming home. It could be whenever I felt like it and for whatever reasons compelled me. If now was not the time, there would be a time. I didn't need to feel guilty toward Clarissa.

I struck wood for close to an hour and then we stopped for another smoke. "What we believe in," Grandpa was saying, more to my Uncle Jason than to me—for some reason in one of his talkative moods—"is the sun, because its journey is quite a bit like our own. It comes up and it goes down and we see it and we know, then, that there is a double meaning in all of life."

I've never been much of a talker so I just kept on chopping wood, pulling dried limbs from the sand along the beach, knocking off the brittle parts. This is the kind of wood that will burn like paper, I thought in a more realistic mood, but it's good for kindling. Right then I knew I was in the cycle of moving away, and even though, to Grandpa, my coming back for good was inevitable and even predestined, at that moment I was not so sure. Should have known then, though, that like the rivers of the world, people, too, move out and come back and move out and come back. Maybe that's what the old man was counting on.

I didn't say anything in response, but was grateful for the old gent's wisdom. I'm lucky to have listened all my life to old men like that, and I take it to mean that anything is possible. I always have a good feeling here where every move made in the universe is accounted for, at least for fleeting moments. Every day the sun goes down, I guess, it goes through the ground and it impregnates the earth. It does its part and that's what people have to do, too.

The steady sound of my ax striking the fragile wood had rung hollowly into that night, and the old man had finally fallen silent. Doing your part is a big deal for the men I've known all my life. Yet, the real world intrudes. Clarissa's pleas seem to go unanswered while I'm wasting away emptying bedpans and changing hospital gowns on the ailing people of an uncaring community.

The old man has invested everything he has in the notion that I will not forget. The land stolen from us by pilgrims and pioneers and politicians is not being returned, and the river, now stained by the sabotage for irrigators and power brokers and dams and civil engineers, is seemingly forever impeded from its natural life. The part human beings must play in this world seems only a vague promise. Not at that moment, but later when I reflected on it all, I had no illusions except to acknowledge that emptying the shit from the bedpans of the infirm was probably not going to do anything for my future . . . just fuel my cynicism.

My Uncle Jason and I loaded the wood. By then darkness had settled on the landscape and the light from the moon streamed over us. I heard the faint sounds of little birds settling down, glad that we were leaving so silence could fill their places and they could get some sleep. This time of night was always a little sad as you looked out on the shining water, the ripples, and the sound of night movements. I wanted to look forward to leaving in the morning bright and early, but was drawn by some instinctive emotion to the sounds of night along the shore, which were anything but unpleasant. In my confused way, I wanted to stay here forever, yet couldn't wait to leave.

We helped the old man step up and heave his old body into the pickup, and we put his walking stick in beside him. The moon shone and we drove along the silvery river to the Big Pipe place, as we had done hundreds of times before.

CHAPTER 6

"**B**y accident!" Clarissa's voice was still ringing in my ears. "That's the way you always do things!"

Her voice had been accusing and she seemed more disgruntled than usual. It's an unfortunate fact of my life that this woman's maternal admonitions won't go away, no matter how hard I try to ignore them. I don't seem to have my grandfather's curious, smiling, grave way of turning her anger and contempt and curses into whatever it is that goes in one ear and out the other. Truth is, my responsibility to him was her powerful plea.

"By accident," she'd repeated in a voice both unbelieving and filled with disgust, not mentioning what she knew was at the heart of it.

Looked like this could have turned into another yelling match.

She had looked at me hard that day, as though trying to intimidate me or figure out how to get me to do what she wanted. I knew that look well and saw it as a confirmation of our endless battles for supremacy.

"Everything is always 'by accident' with you!!"

"No," I had said then, not because I wanted to argue but because I wanted to defend myself from her vicious condemnation, no fantastic visions presenting themselves. Just plodding on trying to manage her anger, not turning back as I often did with Clarissa, just kind of a pitiful response in the face of a long history of her disapproval.

"Just because I'm doing my thing with no particular destination in mind," I'd said with a shrug, "that doesn't mean that I'm not going someplace . . . doesn't mean I won't get someplace. Eventually."

I had laughed it off then, and she, aware that something was different this time, headed for the door.

I followed her.

"Hey, where'd you get the rig?"

She drove off without answering, her feel-nothing, I-don't-give-a-shit look conveying her particular contempt for me and, oddly, for herself.

I had no regrets at seeing her leave, but I didn't know what to think about that conversation in retrospect even after my talk with the old man.

I remember walking slowly to my car, half remembering that I had several books flung in the back seat and had to get them back to the library before they were overdue. I'd circled back to the parking lot wishing morosely that I could compete somehow with Clarissa's anger and condescension. She was a strange woman, seldom determining anything by reason, always by contest, always in a struggle for mastery.

By accident?

What did she mean by that? Accident? I tried to shrug off her words, but I had driven down the street not seeing anything, just in a silent wonderment.

When I got back to work later, I had even more reason to remember Clarissa's words about how accidental my life seemed to be, as Sister Amabolis, red-faced and excited, met me at the door saying she had some information for me. She gestured for me to follow her and we hurried down the hall to her office to retrieve the afternoon's mail.

Robert, who always knew everything that happened at the hospital, appeared out of nowhere, and as we walked, he told me that the old-young woman with the dark grin had included me in her last will and testament. He could hardly contain his excitement, nodding his head over and over again and gesturing.

At first I thought it was a joke, and I was smiling at his enthusiasm. Later, when I found out I really was included in her will, I thought it was money she had given me, but then was told she had given me an heirloom from a collection of Indian artifacts which had been in her family for over a hundred years.

I was stunned.

"An heirloom?" I asked Robert. "What the hell is an heirloom?"

"Well, it's a thing that has been in the family. It's a family possession."

"Yeah? Whose family?"

"Hers, I guess. For a hundred years!"

"A hundred years!"

"Yeah. Isn't that amazing?"

"Jeez."

"Well," Robert went on, ever the know-it-all. "I guess you would call it, in this case, an artifact."

"Oh."

"Yeah. It's something from your people, I think. You know, Indian artifacts are really worth a lot of money these days!"

Do you want to call this an accident? Hey, Clarissa! How about this? Accident? Destiny? An accidental good fortune? Bad fortune? Unexpected? An accident? An accident?

How do you define accidental? Isn't an accident some event that usually results in loss, damage, injury? This isn't any of those things! Maybe "fortuitous" is what is meant here. Are accidental and fortuitous the same thing? Maybe I have to go get a dictionary. Isn't an accident like something that happens without cause? Like . . . like . . . something like . . . meteors falling to the earth? Is that an accident?

Can such an event be called an accident? Or does it have purpose and therefore isn't accidental. Isn't it the purpose of meteors to give signals and meaning to the universe? This was like a meteor, something falling from the sky right into my lap!!

Surely, though, this falling on me of what everyone, including myself, assumed was good fortune from a woman for whom I had felt nothing except a strong dislike, which eventually turned into a vague pity, seemed to be an accident. Meaningless. Without purpose. This awful woman, enmeshed in her own self-centered web so long and so relentlessly that her husband's sorrow drove him to an act of unbearable violence, seemed unable to give meaning to anything in this world. Yet . . . maybe . . .

Maybe to see my world as Clarissa had seen it, a series of strange, dancing roads and inexplicable accidents, wasn't all there was to it. Robert and I and Sister Amabolis looked at the paper that said the woman had made a gift of a family heirloom to me, and we stared at one another not knowing what to say.

I remember how she always called me "the Indian." Every time she saw me she watched me at my work. "You're an Indian, aren't you?"

She would ask that during the moments when she was able to be aware of what was going on around her. I had thought it was because I was the first and only Indian she had ever seen, but maybe she was thinking even then about the gift.

Time kind of stopped for me that day, as we turned the paper over to one another, each looking at it, conscious of the other's presence. I stayed in the hospital after my shift like I was waiting for something; sat around the lounge and drank coffee like I was waiting for the clock to run down and tell me something about this odd event. I looked toward the hallway where I had last seen the stricken husband and tried to remember the woman he loved, the woman whose gift I was to receive. I tried to think kindly of her, as a woman I could admire and be grateful to. I could not.

Instead of seeing her as a woman of generosity, I held on to the image of her struggling to get out of bed only to fall in a heap on the floor, her head hitting hard and saliva spewing. After that she had to be watched night and day. It was then I had realized she could no longer cry, just as she could no longer love, and I saw her hands clawing at anything within reach, her eyes whirling crazily and her body like ice. The hairs on her lip and chin could no longer be removed and her face glistened with sweat. But none of it filled me with any compassion for her. I simply couldn't stand her.

I sat in the lounge waiting for Sister Amabolis to come back from her inner office, where she had gone to make a copy of the letter. She was going to keep a copy for her records and give me the original. Robert, always the nosy one, joined me. He couldn't stand not knowing what I was going to do.

"I can't understand any of this, " I said.

When an orderly shoving a cart before him brought in some flowers and put them in an elegant, swooping vase, I couldn't take my eyes off of him. He went over to the windowsill and began watering the plants there, being particularly careful not to spill over onto the shiny, dark wood. Robert and I, saying nothing to each other, watched him, each with our own thoughts. The orderly's actions seemed so purposeful. Nothing accidental here, I thought. That's why he's called an orderly, hunh? Following ceaseless patterns has always kept the world in shape, even though, to me, it has seemed to be such a sacrifice.

"It's not money," I told Robert. "Don't people usually leave money when they die?"

"Usually. This is something else. A treasured thing, I guess."

"I wonder what it is."

"Well, it's probably the same as money. It's probably pretty valuable."

After a few moments, he continued: "If it is of great value, you know, the husband will not let it stand. You'll have to fight it out, in court, probably. You should get a lawyer."

I looked over at him and he seemed quite serious about his prediction.

"Just in case, you know. I'll go with you to the courthouse," he volunteered quickly.

I looked at him again, disbelieving, and wondered why he felt the need to go with me. It's like the first time I went to the bank to deposit my check from work, and when I told the clerk my name was Big Pipe she took the pen and paper and filled in the blanks for me, like maybe I couldn't do it myself. Like I needed help to do the simplest things. When I asked to use the phone she dialed the number for me.

Now, after weeks of ignoring me, Robert was being solicitous and caring. His behavior griped the shit out of me because he just seemed too phony, so helpful and aiding. But, I just let it go. There's nothing like a little money, or something they think is worth money, to make some people take notice, I thought. Maybe I ought to have been grateful for his help, but hey, I just couldn't force myself. When he reminded me that I might have to testify about what I saw and what I knew about the woman's "suspicious" death, I didn't answer. We sat in stony silence until the mother superior came down the hall and into the waiting room with papers.

"I don't know why the letter was sent here," she said.

"Probably because I don't really have an address," I explained. "So it is difficult to send me anything. No mailing address." I shrugged. "This is the first time I've gotten any mail since I've been here."

Sister took the letter of notification from me and handed me some other papers, all the while peering at us over her eyeglasses.

"Is Robert going with you?"

"No," I said at the same moment Robert said "yes."

"You'd better hurry. You're supposed to be there in an hour."

"You should get a lawyer," Robert said again, this time with what I took to be exaggerated authority, as we left the hospital and walked hurriedly to the parking lot. "You know, some good legal advice."

He couldn't get the passenger-side door of the Limo open, so I got in and reached across the front seat and gave the door a couple of good whacks. He opened the loosened door like he was handling fire, got in, and we rattled on down the street. I punched Scabby Robe's *Powwow Songs* into the tape player, and the drum and the high-pitched sounds of Plains Indian songs filled the air. Robert looked over at me like I was from another planet.

"You like that?" I asked, grinning, turning it up just a bit.

He was speechless.

"Some of these guys used to sing with the Halfway-Up-South-Hill-Drum, but that outfit never made any tapes," I told him, as though he could give a shit. He looked helpless and awkward and I liked that.

"Now they call themselves Crown Butte."

"Oh," he managed.

The sounds of Indian singing filled the air, and I alternately watched the speedometer and Robert out of the corner of my eye and we said nothing more.

Now it was their move, I thought as we made our way up the steps of the Clay County Courthouse. When I saw the husband looking at me, I looked away. I applied myself conscientiously to filling out the long lists of questions they gave me, and the husband came over and said, "I'm glad you're here."

"Uh . . . thanks."

We sat at the bench across from the desk and he said, "Did you know that my stepchildren are contesting the will?"

"No."

"Well, unfortunately they are. My wife was quite well off, you know. Her family owned a lot of real estate here, and her father was head of the medical school here."

I waited for him to finish.

"And her children by a previous marriage, well, you know they don't . . ." As he started to explain, his whole face trembled. "They don't . . . um-m-m . . . don't . . ." He couldn't finish and put his head in his hands.

I was paralyzed with the sudden fear that he was going to weep right there in front of me, become a slobbering idiot, confess, cause a huge public commotion; but he pulled himself together, grabbed a handkerchief from his coat pocket, and dabbed at his eyes.

This decent man had suffered with the old-young addict whose life was damaged beyond most human endurances, and I had witnessed that suffering. I had seen his suffering. It was real. And although I hadn't predicted what it was going to cost him, I knew all along, even from the beginning, that I should have . . . I should have . . . been more help. The children he spoke of had never come to the hospital to visit her, as far as I knew, yet here he was now sitting and telling me how they wanted to cash in on their mother's death. Maybe they had that right, but I felt great pity for the man.

It's a common occurrence, I suppose, in a world where the only thing that matters is money, that once a person is dead the people who have grown to despise or resent the deceased crawl out of their monotonous lives and reveal their smallness.

Robert hung around, stood on one foot and then the other right behind my chair, serious and anxious at the same time, like one of those fickle prairie skies that can't make up its mind whether to fade away in the wind or let it all go, drenching everything in sight. Clearing his throat, peering into the folders on the table, trying to hear what was being said, he wanted some attention. Even he, though, seemed to feel uneasy in the presence of this awful moment of emotional display by the husband. Tactfully, for once, he kept quiet.

After what seemed like many long minutes of silence, the husband moved his papers, shoved them over to the man in the blue suit who was with him, and said, "Well, I guess this is over with for now . . . it's time to go."

"Yeah," I agreed.

Blue Suit shoved the papers into a leather briefcase. They would let us know about the date for further court dealings, we were told by the clerk at the window.

We all straggled toward the doors, uncomfortable and quiet. I felt better about the husband, though, and I think he felt better about me. I wondered if Robert was a bit disappointed that we weren't going to have to "fight it out," as he had predicted.

We left the building and drove away, the husband with Blue Suit in his BMW and Robert and me in my Limo, none of us knowing what the judge would have to say. I didn't know if I would have to testify or who the witnesses were, nor did I know if a crime had been committed or if this was going to just be an estate hearing.

I still didn't know what the "heirloom" was or what the "artifact" was. Unknowingness, like the gray sky hanging over us ceaselessly, would have to be endured, for how long I couldn't say. In the car, encased from the chill of the day, Robert seemed like an alien being, and I couldn't wait to drop him off at the hospital steps.

So this is what accidental is? How could it be accidental when I felt the threat of memory so near? The vast prairie people "making it to Canada," like the *keyapi* stories say. There may have been no artifacts of those events in real terms but plenty of stories in imaginative terms. The stories have told us about the trees along the creek; my grandpa, walking slowly to the corral to speak to the gelding before putting a saddle on him, told us of how it was for all of them, the survivors of a terrible history.

So now, a "thing"—who knows what it is—an artifact, as Robert had described it. Does this mean something made by "your people," as he also was describing it? So near and yet so far. Something hidden in the gray sky closed in on me and I couldn't say why I felt so alone.

After Robert hustled up the steps, I remembered the books in the back seat of my car and, shaking off the silence of the moment, decided to drive to the library. If it was still open I would stay awhile. Knowing about this insatiable appetite for books I've had all my life, I knew I would be comforted in their midst.

CHAPTER 7

In the hours and days that passed after hearing of my "accidental" good fortune, I was neither irritated nor pacified by what was a clear motivation on the part of the old-young woman to aspire to whatever kindness she could give at what was a final stage of her disintegration.

"Don't think I'm a mind reader," I said to some of the staff who kept asking what the gift was.

"But, don't you have some idea?"

"Nope . . . not a clue."

Truth is, I thought about her and the gift less and less as I simply got back to work. It was my habit to just go from one day to the next, no need to spend a lot of time worrying, no need to give any thought to what might be called a concealed or hidden human life. Who had any notion of what other people were up to, anyway? More to the point, who cared?

Immediately, and probably not unexpectedly, things at the hospital changed drastically. I was abruptly transferred to the psychiatric ward because Robert, now a head nurse on the floor, was still suspicious of me, didn't know what to think of me or where I stood on matters he'd already taken a stand on. The nuns just wanted to know if I was going to get any money. I told them I wasn't sure what was happening but that I didn't think it involved money.

"You're probably going to do okay here," Sister Amabolis said as she walked with me to my new assignment. She was a kind and caring woman, always trying to reassure me. As I strode beside her I watched her large black shoes, conspicuous under the white starched habit she wore, taking strong measure of her journey, silently, purposefully. Size tens. Maybe even elevens, I thought as I watched them make their way down the hall beside me. They made no sound, but her heavy skirt swished and her rosary beads hanging from her waist rattled cheerfully with every muted step.

Stupidly—and, as usual, with little or no forethought—I agreed that I'd probably do okay, but that was before I knew where I was being transferred. If it wasn't the cuckoo's nest, it was damn near. It really didn't matter where I was, though. I was only an aide, after all, and all I did was empty bedpans and clean up the units and sterilize the utensils and give people baths and take their temperatures and blood pressure. I could do that in the psych ward as well as anyplace else.

The first time I walked down the hall, on my very first day at my new assignment, I was startled out of my doldrums by a guy with the d.t.'s, gasping and screeching and rushing down the hall, hollering some unintelligible warnings to stay away from him, close to tears, purple-faced, nonsensical. He had escaped his room, wild-eyed, his hair standing out like he'd just taken a thousand volts.

A frightened but determined little nurse, her cap askew and her arms flailing, followed him out the door as he hurled an empty aluminum urinal toward her, knocking a window in the door loose.

"Hey," she hollered. "Grab him."

"Hunh?"

"Grab him!"

Instinctively, I put out my arms like I was catching horses at the corral, and as he came toward me I suddenly realized I knew him.

"Hey, Allie," I said, recognizing an old friend from Stephan mission school. "Hey ... hey ... hey—"

But before another word left my mouth, he pushed me up against the wall and threw a left hook that knocked me cold.

I remembered nothing for a little while.

I stayed home the next day and ended up nursing a sore jaw and a black eye for about a week. The old guys in the ward got a big charge out of my situation.

"Whaddya doin', chief . . . you been on the warpath?"

Jeez, if they only knew what I was thinking.

Maintaining, I said only, "Go back to your Ole and Lena jokes, guys," but I was curious about who was responsible for the entire fiasco.

In the hospital's efforts to handle the situation that day of Allie's escape, they had killed him, and it was only after I got back that I found out.

It was the first time ever that I had gotten close enough to how white people handle out-of-control Indians to know the truth. I probably know a lot of out-of-control Indians, and I'd been in a lot of out-of-control situations over the years, but this time it was different. Allie wasn't breaking any laws, after all. He was no terrorist . . . no AIM militant. Just a guy in a fruitless attempt to save himself from whatever danger he found himself in.

As it turned out, they were using me as a prime example to show how out of control he was, and they paid a lot of attention to my black eye and scraped-up elbows, even taking pictures of the bruises.

"After he knocked you out," Robert told me, "and while he was being restrained by hospital staff, they had to call the police. From downtown. Law enforcement officers from the City PD."

"What'd they do then?" I asked.

"They had to spray him with mace," Robert said excitedly. "Man, he was out of it! He trashed a couple of examining rooms before they got him. They beat him with their batons, shackled him, and left him on the floor to 'cool off.'"

"How long?"

"Hunh?"

"How long was he there? On the floor?"

"I don't know."

No one seemed to know. So, in the few moments of my lunch hour that first day I was back at work, I went into the records room and looked at the chart that hadn't yet been sent to the permanent files. Four hours! He was there unattended from 6:15 until after 10:00 before they checked on him again. Just as I was leaving the records room, one of the RNs came in and was surprised to see me there. She asked, "What are you doing in here?"

"Nothing," I replied hurriedly. "Nothing. Wrong place. Sorry."

I slipped out smiling, but I had found what I was curious about. Four hours!

I couldn't believe it. This was a hospital, wasn't it? Where they were supposed to care for you? Make you well? Allie, a guy I knew from school, suffered . . . ?

... a cardiac arrest? ... and died? ... how? ... an accident? Are they going to call this an accident? How many more accidents can I take? Allie was a young guy, hardly a candidate for cardiac arrest. I hadn't known Allie all that well because he was a few years behind me in boarding school. I remember him as a skinny little boy then, but he sure grew into a big, hulking guy, the sort who could knock you out with one punch.

One time, I remembered, at a school basketball game there was some scuffling and loud swearing between the two teams, and Allie ran out on the court and separated a couple of guys who had started it. Otherwise he just seemed to hang around the ping-pong tables watching people play and trying to get some bets going. He never talked much, and it seemed like he never wanted to listen, either.

He died sometime during those four hours, no one seemed to know exactly when. All alone and unattended for a very long time. Too long, I thought to myself. Emergency efforts to revive him were unsuccessful, Robert told me, and Allie was pronounced dead at 11:09 that night. Official.

It was pathologist Brad Randall, who came in from the capital city, who put forward the official interpretation of the events. He reported that Allie's death was a death by "Accidental Positional Asphyxiation," or APA as he glibly described it. It seemed to me that he was using words to put the best face on what most people would call an abuse of force by medical attendants and the police. The pathologist went on in his most officious manner saying that APA sometimes occurs in individuals "who are unable to breathe normally because of an excited state, body positions, and other conditions."

Body position? Other conditions? How about calling it a choke hold, I thought when I heard this explanation. Anybody who has been in any barroom scuffle knows what a choke hold is ... it's an offensive maneuver used to overpower and sometimes kill somebody when you can't use a gun.

But because Randall held in his hand the written word, the written report, the final proof of legitimacy, I imagined that the hospital staff and the doctors and the investigators, all good and honorable men and women, would make sure the words "choke hold" would never be used to describe what went on that night.

Captain Chris Grant of the City PD and Clay County Sheriff's office was already completing the investigation when I got to work bright and early Tuesday. At the A.M. meeting of the staff which was called by the fearful ... and responsible ... sisters who ran the place, we were told standard procedure in cases like this was that finds are to be turned over to the State Department of Criminal Investigation for independent review, and we were assured that everything had been done appropriately.

The little nurse, now subdued and clinical, sat beside me at the long, official-looking table.

"I'm Claire," she said, "Claire Smith."

I moved and shook hands with her rather formally.

"Thanks," I whispered. "Thanks a lot, Claire Smith."

She looked puzzled.

"You know," I said, sitting there with my wounded face, "Hey, hey . . . stop him, grab him!?'"

I gestured.

She laughed.

The meeting went on. "Our investigation has not revealed any indication that this event is criminal in nature," the CPD told the nuns.

I wasn't surprised, but I wondered what the state DCI would be able to find out. Everyone at the hospital seemed to be closing ranks, I thought. I was standing on the outside east patio of the hospital with a can of cola a bit later when I saw Dorothy, Allie's sister. It was dusk the very day the City PD and county investigators were rendering their verdict of no responsibility.

As the sun drained itself from the heavy sky, I watched Dorothy, whom I hadn't seen since boarding school, with a mixture of concern and puzzlement as she walked up the steps of the hospital carrying a wide bundle. I later learned that was the clothing and the short boots her brother had worn at admission to his deadly hospital stay. That's all that remained for her of him. Her shoulders were slumped as though giving full weight to her kind of suffering which compelled her to visit the site of her brother's struggle for life.

I hadn't seen her in years, but I knew immediately she was conducting her own investigation into the abuses everyone knew but kept under wraps. A really skinny little guy of six or seven, her son, looking much like the Allie I had known years ago, trailed behind her.

"Albert," she admonished quietly as she gestured toward him to hurry up, "*hi-nah-hi-ni.*"

I drained the can of Coke, tossed it into the bin marked "Waste," and out of curiosity followed her through the doorway. Convinced that those who had been in charge of saving her younger brother had, instead, murdered him, she seemed purposeful. She simply nodded to me and walked up to the nurse's station and said, "I am the sister of Allen Eagle and I want to see where you killed him."

Without a moment's hesitation, the desk nurse corrected her. "You must mean that you are here to see where he suffered a heart attack."

"I know what happened," Dorothy said accusingly, probably recognizing in the immediate response the fear.

The nurse, meticulous in her starched uniform, looked down at her papers and in her formal way said stiffly, "There is no need to—"

"You think I'm being hysterical?"

"No," the nurse said slowly, as though talking to a recalcitrant child. "I just think you're overreacting."

"He's dead!" Dorothy moaned and leaned against the station. The little guy looked on, wide-eyed.

The nurse looked at me and made a slight motion.

"Just because he had looks like a beggar and his hair is long and tangled and you think he's an Indian out of control, it's okay that you took him down?" Dorothy asked, the anguish clear in her voice. "The . . . the . . . police . . . and the nurses . . . they . . . they can tie him up and . . . and . . . leave him to die alone?"

Her voice was suddenly muted. "He . . . he . . . couldn't breathe, don't you understand? He couldn't get his breath."

She was right, of course. Even the little nurse, Claire Smith, had described the incident this way. They were all stricken with fear, the nurse had said to the investigators, and while they were trying to subdue him somebody ran and called security and within minutes the city police brought mace and batons and beat him down. In fact, Nurse Smith told me she had read the report that indicated that after they had subdued him, they left him trussed up "like a stuck pig," she said, on the cement floor of an empty examining room for hours.

Others who were present said he was bleeding from the nose and mouth and from cuts on his head, and they said his blood made a huge puddle where he was lying. They said by the time the badly beaten body was removed, the blood was coagulated like Jell-O on the gray surface.

Dorothy stood for a long time at the counter, tying and untying some strings from her dead brother's sweater. She began to cry again and her tears ran down her cheeks like rainfall. Oh, god, she said. She clutched the boots tightly.

None of this grief was recorded in a police report. In fact, nothing was ever made public about any of this. And, to this day I think much of the evidence and information about the whole thing remains sealed.

CHAPTER 8

"How'd you get here?"

"Hitched."

"That must have taken a while, huh?"

I looked at Albert and realized that this was a small brown-skinned boy who had learned early the answers to a hard life's questions.

She looked down at him and drew him to her and kissed him on the forehead, pushing his long black hair out of his eyes.

"Yeah. A couple of days. Nobody picks anybody up anymore."

"Too many serial killers on the road, I guess."

"Hunh? Do I look like a serial killer?"

"No. No. I meant . . . ," laughing.

She didn't give the Limo a second glance, waited for Albert to get in the back seat, slammed the door hard and got in, put the boots and sweater down by her feet, and punched up the powwow tape like she belonged there.

"It was good to walk, though," she said in an attempt at uplifting her trembling voice. She looked out of the side window blind to the flimsy bridges next to the interstate, the small rusty silos built next to huge abandoned grain elevators now gray with disuse and neglect, the old cars, unpainted houses lining the highway.

"I could have walked forever," she said wistfully. "And we just got so tired and just kept on going."

Her shiny black hair hung over her face, and she slumped in the seat and then threw her head back and said in an agonized voice, "It has been so sad, Philip. So sad, for all of us. You should see my mom. She's never going to get over this." She covered her eyes. "Poor Allie. Poor Allie."

Lucky it was quittin' time because it was a four-hour drive to her folks' place, and we just settled in the best we could, though the Limo is anything but comfortable. There was little traffic on I-90, mostly eighteen-wheelers, and the flat fields were colorless and wasted, like the somber scenes in a foreign film. The western sky was gray and colorless, too, making the drive unpleasant and tedious.

After an hour or so, with Albert sacked out in the back seat, we decided to stop at the next town. We took the rough ramp off the freeway in search of a cup of coffee. There were no immediate food places so we drove slowly through the streets until we found ourselves on the street where the "*only Corn Palace in the known world*" stands full of neon lights and tourist trash. We ordered coffee, and just as we walked around the corner carrying paper cups, we heard the sounds of people talking, muffled laughter.

Turning, we saw a whole bunch of Indians sitting next to the outer wall in the partly shaded alley. Side by side. They looked like part of the building's mural made up of dark figures, corncobs, and geometric designs—an Indian pastoral of sorts. They didn't pay any attention to us but kept up their joking and laughing, quietly and with a great sense of fun. They were passing around a bottle. We sat down with them.

Dorothy was quiet, deep in her own thoughts. Eavesdropping, we listened to an old man tell his woman companion that her hands were beautiful. She, her graying hair and her sagging skin on her face telling of hard times and the passing of many years, put her head down and smiled, revealing her missing teeth. They both looked at her hands, rough and big, the nails ragged and dirty. She leaned against him and murmured something we couldn't hear and took his hand in hers, and he laughed. Dorothy, her arm around Albert, looked down at him and they both smiled.

Later the old man began to sing. It was an odd song and I wondered if I'd ever heard it before. He sang quietly. His voice was muffled but I could make out a few words: *wi-ya wan tewahila k'un.* I knew then as I listened that he was Oglala, or maybe from Rosebud. What was he singing? *There was a woman I loved so dearly?* Is that what he is saying? I whispered to Dorothy. She shrugged and sipped her coffee and looked out on the empty street.

I had forgotten it was Sunday and that's why almost everything was closed down and there was so little traffic in the streets. This was a white man's church-going community, huge spires of stone churches in the distance, churches that had been here over a hundred years.

Somehow, the man's singing depressed us both. Why did we feel bad? It was a happy song, wasn't it? It was about the love of a woman, wasn't it? I looked over at Dorothy and it was like everything stopped. The air was still, and my eyes felt like they were suddenly filled with cotton. She was close, so familiar, her skin so clear and her eyes dark, unfathomable.

Our relatives were a part of the landscape here and I saw them in her chiseled face. The Yanktons. The Santees. The Hunkpati. They had loved one another here, married and had families and made their homes along the creeks here. Looking away, I stared up at the gathering white clouds.

I was struck by how accidental it all was, just like Clarissa said. Here we were sitting together by mere chance, purely by chance, trying to hear an old Sioux man sing a strange song in the shade of one of the strangest buildings on earth, a corn palace made by white immigrant people in the 1930s.

Dorothy will go back home, I mused silently, and I will return to the hospital, and both of us will know what we've always known, that the road stretches endlessly on. I felt suddenly like I didn't want the road to be an endless and useless thing; I wanted to see the horses prancing on that road, silent and colorful and filled with meaning.

Leaning closer I said, "After great hardship and grief, and . . . whatever . . . it is ironic, isn't it, that we all meet accidentally in places like this." Looking around at our anonymous companions and breaking a moment of stunning, breathless recognition that anything was possible, I asked, "Don't you think so?"

"Yeah," she said smiling. "Yeah . . . in a crazy place like this, in the bright streets of a prairie town like this." She looked around.

Albert got up, got some coins from his mother, and left to find some candy and something to drink.

"Don't get lost, Albert," his mother called after him. "And come right back, okay?"

He didn't answer but went around the corner.

"This is a strange place," I said looking out at the iron gateway, the entrance to the Corn Palace.

"Yeah," she agreed. "Have you ever seen those designs in there?" She gestured toward the building.

I shook my head.

"They decorated the ceilings, floors, and borders with the Nazi swastikas, and ever since they've been calling them Indian designs."

"Have you been here before?"

"Uh-huh. I guy I knew from home, from the Agency, who did Indian dancing for the tourists here brought his whole family and danced here . . . for the tourists . . . every summer."

I laughed.

"No, really," she said nodding, "And one time we came here to see him. My folks. And all of us . . . Allie . . ." She looked away.

"Jeez. I've never been here, but I've always heard about the Corn Palace. I was told that a famous Indian artist, Oscar Howe, did some designing here."

"Yeah . . . well he didn't do the swastikas. They did that much earlier than when he worked here."

"The Palace of Corn." I heard myself imitate Johnny Carson giving some kind of dismissive tone.

"Here we are," I said then—turning on my best performance voice, important, grandiose, like I was talking on the radio—"in the shade of a . . . a . . . cultural edifice . . . which brings meaning into . . . which brings meaning to Euro-American incursions into—"

She burst out laughing, and as she did I noticed some of the others watching us. I decided to quit showing off, to talk Indian the rest of the time so we wouldn't become so noticeable. English is always so loud. But, we were already noticeable, I suppose, as the youngest by many decades of the whole group. And probably the best dressed, though I may have flattered us, this being probably a matter of taste.

We sat there throughout the afternoon enjoying just being together, two lonesome and isolated people, I suppose, hardly able to believe our good luck at seeing one another again. Neither of us talked all that much, but even our silences and haphazard bits of casual conversation seemed like confidences I'd not shared with anyone in a long time.

Albert came back and spent his time sitting on the curb, waiting and soaking up the sun. He seemed like a patient little boy. One of the women next to the wall called him over and tried to give him some gum, but he shook his head.

"Maybe you knew him, too." Dorothy ventured.

"Who?"

"The Indian dancer."

"Oh. I don't know. Maybe."

"It was a guy they called Hepana. He was Wahpeton."

"Oh, sure. Sure. I knew him. He was about forty?"

"Uh-huh."

"He was a great dancer! Well known by everybody."

"He was from Sisseton, wasn't he?"

"Well, originally, I guess. But he lived at the Fort for a long time."

After a pause she said, "You know, I've always been curious about this place . . . this corn palace."

"Why is that?"

"Don't you think it is interesting that it is decorated with corn made into the swastika by immigrant people to this region?"

"Oh. Well, I didn't know it was, until now. Is it really?"

"Yes." She nodded, enthusiastic now. "You just have to take my word for it. It was! And what I know about that kind of history of this place, in the 1930s or so, there was some kind of organization, I think it was called the American Federation, and it was full of white people—and remember this was after World War I with Germany and before World War II with Germany, and there's lots of Germans around here." She swept her arms out grandly. "And this organization . . . it wasn't Indian at all. It was white people and they wanted to help Indians. They got organized so they could oppose the Indian Reorganization Act."

I raised my eyebrows.

"I'll say that again,"—her voice now sounding conspiratorial—"they opposed the Indian Reorganization Act!"

"Who were these people?" I was thinking how smart she was and wondered how she knew these things.

"Well, I don' know, exactly. But you know there was a lot of organizing around here in those days, labor unions and farmers unions and all that. It was in the middle of the Depression, you know."

"Yeah."

"And so, people were organizing, even around here," she gestured, "in this godforsaken place. I think they were mostly religious fundamentalists—you know, the kind that always want to do something Christian to help the Indians. Not many Indians around here joined into that kind of thing, but there were a lot of Creeks and Choctaws who got interested. They called Collier and the Roosevelt New Deal and all that "fascist," and they said that the Indians would suffer if the policies were reorganized, and any new kind of tribal government, especially a modern one, was a bad thing."

"All this is very interesting, Dorothy . . . and, for sure, it's news to me. But, what are you getting at?"

"My point is I've always wondered about it."

"What do you mean?"

"Well, I really don't know, but I've always been struck by the use of the swastika on this building and inside of it."

"Yeah . . . the Sioux don't use the design backward like the swastika is. But, say, don't the Navajo use it backwards?"

"I don't know, but here, in the middle of Sioux Country? Why? I asked my folks about it when I was taking some college classes at that community college in Bismarck, North Dakota. I tried to get some people to talk about it, even wrote some letters to the editor, but nobody was intrigued about it like I was. German immigrants were a big deal around here, you know, and they still are. I wonder what they know about it. They and the Catholic Church practically made this town what it is."

"I didn't know you went to school in Bismarck."

"Yeah. At United Tribes Tech."

"But," I said, turning the talk back to the corn designs, "don't they say around here that it is an Indian design?"

"Well, sure . . . you think they're going to admit it is a Nazi design? Look at it sometime and you'll see what it is. It's a German design, not Indian. Nazi!!"

"Are you saying these people around here are, or were, Nazis?"

She threw back her head and laughed.

"I don't know what I'm saying."

She leaned over and dug a cigarette from the pack in my shirt pocket. I flipped on my lighter. Her hands cupped mine and I saw how slim and small her hands were. She wore a red coral ring on her left hand. I wondered if there was somebody special who had given it to her. Her eyes did not meet mine so I didn't ask.

We sat together; our deep personal thoughts seemed shared and convivial. I remembered the same design on the inside floor of a famous old-time hotel in downtown Rapid City. I thought . . . you know, we could become conspiracy buffs, and I smiled at the thought. At least we got Dorothy's mind off her grief for a few minutes.

It was getting very late. Some of the people sitting next to us left, and others came, and finally, with great reluctance, I got up, held out my hand, and helped her to her feet.

Suddenly, she put her arms around my waist and we stood there and she held on tight. She was so small. I felt her breath come in great gasps as we stood for several long minutes.

We got to her parents' place about two o'clock in the morning, and forgetting about my foolish vows of celibacy, I stayed with her that night, and I held her and felt perhaps for the first time ever that the elk dancers might be watching us, but I wasn't afraid. I wondered if she felt their eyes on us, but I didn't ask about that either. The fewer questions at this point the better, I decided.

In the morning I felt giddy as I dressed quickly and made my way through the clothes and shoes scattered on the floor. I wished I had something I could leave for her and the boy, but I had nothing to give.

I left before anyone got up, put on my dark glasses, and drove into the dawn. The river looked cool and calm as I drove along its edge on the bumpy reservation road, and the hills in the distance seemed closer than I remembered them. I made my way to the highway, the horses prancing on the chaotic road in front of me.

CHAPTER 9

For a couple of weeks I was really distracted by the promise that I might see her again, but I did nothing to contact her. Maybe I expected her to show up again on her own. After that night, though, I felt really alone again, a feeling less random than ever before because now there was the possibility that this surprising meeting was no accident.

It was the quietness of our time together that I valued, the feeling of some kind of vague, common recognition, an indefinable lingering. I watched television, went to work, spent lots of time at the library staring at pages of books; I listened to the radio and at times even read the papers. None of it seemed of interest.

Finally, getting a notice of the courthouse hearing and coming together there with others on a particularly bright day filled with sunshine, I began to pull myself together. I had begun to grasp the fact that I had to think now about how deeply I was drawn into situations that I never could have imagined just a few months ago.

Sitting on a hard bench in the courthouse beside Sister and the ever-present Robert, I had to admit, if to no one but myself, that my life was expanding and getting more complicated than I liked.

"At the time the will is made," the judge was saying at the probate hearing that commenced about midday, "mental capacity must exist, and there is no question that Mrs. Larson knew what she was doing when she gave the museum piece, the collector's item, to Mr. Big Pipe."

When he got to say his piece, the lawyer for the adult children who were protesting this proceeding told the judge in heated language that he had no choice but to deny the gift, that the woman could not be considered a reliable giver, that her gift had to be denied because she had a long history of problems, that her memory had been failing for more years than anyone could count, and at the end she was incoherent and not in her right mind. She was known as a habitual drinker, he said, a helpless alcoholic, and was so addicted to drugs that she could no longer take care of herself.

The judge stared unblinkingly at the children's lawyer, his dark eyes polite but penetrating. He hunched forward and his arms rested heavily on the oak desk. Every now and then his glance flickered toward the rest of us in the room, and I would remember the courtroom scene later as the beginning of my understanding of a calculated strategy that was meant to intimidate all of us and force us to accept whatever decision was handed down. We would, of course, bow to the authority of a system so deliberate and so dense and, for me, so profoundly depressing.

I suddenly felt bone tired, excluded from finding meaning in this dialogue of these participants; in a state of total boredom I began to worry that before this tedious thing was over with I would fall asleep and crash to the floor, embarrassing myself like a clumsy fool. The image of such a catastrophe brought a smile to my lips and I straightened my shoulders and tried again to listen.

The arguments made by the children's lawyer were very convincing, what I could bring myself to listen to, and the questions raised about the woman's competence made perfect sense and were probably essential to making some kind of decent decision. What was being said seemed true enough as far as I knew. How could she have left me a gift of any kind, and especially a gift of historical significance, if she couldn't even remember my name? "Why" was even more of a puzzle. It didn't make sense.

The thought of the woman's pale skin turning dark and rough, the remembered look of anguish in her eyes gave me a feeling of hopelessness and rage. I wanted to get up and walk about the room, read some of the books on the green velvet–lined shelves that surrounded us. There was so much I didn't know, so much that was unexplainable. I felt trapped and wanted to move on and away from this business. I didn't really want the gift anyway, whatever it turned out to be.

For centuries, lawyers, even those early self-taught lawyers from ancient

Greek and Roman civilizations, have used their knowledge and their ability with rhetoric and argument and books like these on these shelves for weapons, and it was hard for me to imagine that anything good could come of all this. These books, it seemed, and the white people who sat around these tables and on these benches surrounded me much like the Western heroes surrounded Indians on television screens, self-centered and shameless and angry.

"But," the judge was saying to the quiet, sullen group gathered round the oak table looking from one dark face to another, including mine, "did she understand the nature of her act, that is the question, and does she know the person to whom she is leaving this special property? And the answer is 'yes' to both inquiries.

"We have gotten the testimony of people who say she knew Mr. Big Pipe and often asked for him by reference to 'the Indian,' and he took care of her for months as a hospital attendant. There is really nothing untoward in this gift."

We sat hunched forward and I took notice of the children, two girls and a boy. The boy sat perched on the edge of the dark wood chair, his thighs flung out in an athletic sprawl like he was pretending to be Sylvester Stallone. His sisters, the young daughters of the deceased, were cutting glances at each other, and they just seemed so self-satisfied, so sure they were going to prove their poor, unfortunate mother a helpless freak unable to make decisions on her own. They didn't look dangerous or threatening, just willful and dogged and mad as hell.

"You know," the judge explained as he looked long and hard at the papers before him, "the capacity for making a will is a different and lower standard of capacity than that required to make a contract."

"Yeah"—Robert leaned over and suddenly, getting rid of his usual Sunday School know-it-all demeanor, whispered in my ear—"the rutabaga standard." And he snorted as though he needed to let out some hostility he had been keeping hidden. I glared at him and wondered why he was so mean-spirited toward a woman he hardly knew. Few white guys get many high marks from me just on general principle, but this guy, Robert, got none. I turned away, unwilling to acknowledge what I supposed was his effort to inject some humor into the somber, tedious, angry proceedings.

"No one except her lawyers and the proper witnesses participated in drafting the will," the judge went on, "so we can't say that there was undue influence by anyone. Mr. Big Pipe, the young Indian male who is to receive the gift, was not in a confidential relationship with the deceased. And her husband is to receive the bulk of her estate in a separate procurement or disbursement. There is no fraud, no deception here, and I find for and with the testator that the testator has made her 'last will and testament' or device in perfectly good faith."

With that the judge and the lawyers and the clerks disappeared into the chambers.

Even as he uttered the words *the testator has made her "last will and testament,"* the children were on their feet, and in an instant I saw again the face of the old-young woman, her lips stretched over her perfect yellow teeth in a grimace meant to be a smile.

The husband followed the children out of the heavy paneled door, stopping them to say, "One day it has to dawn on you that you are completely out of order to shame your mother's memory in this way."

One of the daughters, hurrying out beside her siblings, shouted, "Out of order? Us? Us?"

Her arm went up and she slapped him hard across the face. The husband and those of us watching gasped and Robert shouted, "Wait a minute, here . . ."

Turning to her siblings the daughter said, "Let's get out of here before I do something I shouldn't!!"

"Shit, no," hollered the brother turning back from the door, "we're not leaving until I work this asshole over!," and he grabbed the husband around the neck and put a knee in his back and forced him up against the wall and beat him, powerful punches that happened so quick; threatening and menacing moves like a fighter with nothing to lose; his eyes focused on the husband's shocked face and nothing else. He shoved the husband's head against the wall again and again with great force. It was like he was possessed, the hate-filled expression opening and closing and drawing in the two daughters, who fell to slapping and kicking until the husband was on the floor bleeding.

"Don't, please. Cecil. Andrea." The husband's cry was not of pain, just anguish.

I looked around. Where's the bailiff? Isn't there supposed to be a bailiff here? All I saw was pure fear in the husband's eyes, and I wondered about the previous dealings these people had had with one another. A long history was being confronted here, and those of us who watched had no clue what it meant.

The three perpetrators looked down at the fallen man, yelling and swearing at him. Robert, in a state of shock, could say nothing more, and I stood as if transfixed, not wanting to witness the total humiliation of a man whose life had been a sea of misery for god knows how many years.

"You son of a bitch," cried the young man. "I'll see you dead before I see you get her money!"

The three of them rushed from the room, their shoes clacking down the marble hall.

The husband was sobbing.

"Let me help you," Robert said finally, taking the husband's arms carefully and avoiding the blood which had spilled from his wounds. Robert, ever the caretaker, dug some Kleenex from his pocket and began dabbing at the man's forehead.

The husband tried to stand, his hands holding his bleeding head. There wasn't a guard or a clerk in sight. I looked around the empty hall for a telephone but saw none.

The husband slumped down again and sat there for a long time on the marble floor, his shirt and tie askew, his sparse hair rumpled and eyes slitted, without expression. Robert sat on his haunches beside him unable to say anything.

"I've got the gift in my lawyer's office," the husband said finally in a choked voice, turning back from the door and his disappeared stepchildren.

"I'm sorry about this, but listen"—he was now gathering his senses and turning to the business at hand—"I'll get it and bring it to my home and you can come over and get it. Will sometime next week be okay?"

"Oh, sure," I said, "sure."

I was eager to get out of there and away from these people who apparently had old scores to settle and didn't mind what public places they used to settle them. Indians, I thought, usually go to some less sanctioned places to do their settling of old scores—like behind taverns or in dark alleys. Families fighting and clawing at each other was surely nothing new, but doing it in the public halls of old law buildings seemed particularly tacky. These people are worse than badgers, I thought, those little hard animals that are so quick to defensiveness, which is pretty scary but usually fairly meaningless. Unlike the badger, these people meant business.

We set the time and the battered husband gave me the address of a place on the other side of town.

CHAPTER 10

Every day the following week I sat alone in my room like a man with no phone waiting for the phone to ring. Or a man with no friends listening for a knock on the door. I would go to work leaving the rumpled clothes unattended on the cot where I slept uneasily.

It was a stranger's room with an ugly, meaningless painting on the wall and a skillet filled with leftover fried potatoes on the stove, stained black on the inside. I often sat thankful for nothing but the quiet. I thought of how Dorothy hid her face away from me when we made love that last time, how we would lie quietly without speaking, and how much I needed to see her.

The following week I drove with some apprehension toward the east side of town early in the morning. I located Rural Route 8, and then 3700 on the street signs, and watched a row of aspens lining the driveway of the husband's place slip by my windows, evenly placed in perfect order, like soldiers guarding an estate of importance or an ammunitions area essential to their lives, maybe a road to nowhere. This was a place the old-young woman had once called home, and it seemed to me this road held a hidden landscape and loneliness and pain. Was it always like this?

Whoa, I said out loud, this is the kind of place where you ought to salute somebody! Box hedges were everywhere—at the front door, behind the garage, along the wide porch that wrapped around the three-story brick house.

Like a Victorian edifice in an otherwise unremarkable neighborhood where every house sat alone on at least five acres, the house was imposing in its well-kept landscape and looked like it had been standing there for a couple of hundred years. Black wrought-iron posts held round lighting fixtures that matched the yard furniture.

Full-maned lions of white iron with dark blue marble eyes lay staring at me from the protruding walkways, and a small iron statue of a black stable man guarded the gate. I thought those black livery statues, like Aunt Jemimas, were no longer in good taste since the Black Power movement made white folks feel bad and uncomfortable with their slave imagery. About the time Red Power came about, most people started to get rid of mascots and all that stuff, but I guessed such racial consciousness hadn't made it to these parts.

The minute I stepped out of my car, I regretted my loose gray T-shirt, faded jeans, and scuffed cowboy boots, but I let the husband lead me through the heavy patio doors. I couldn't help noticing the sun streaming through huge bay windows as we entered the library, and thought this was, perhaps, more friendly territory than the exterior—a place meant to be kind of homey, really. Huge, heavy-legged tables and leather chairs stood in front of the bookcases, and lamps were lighted even though the room was filled with natural sunshine.

I was nervous as I looked at the large bundle on one of the oak tables.

The husband asked me to sign a paper, saying, "This is worth thousands of dollars," and as I bent over the table I felt that I was casually being introduced to the museum culture of white folks who rob graves and steal from Indians. I couldn't help feeling a stab of resentment.

When I unwrapped the gift from its very, very old linen wrappings, now turning to parchment, I felt like I was handling something very precious. The husband stood too close and I moved away a bit. He touched my shoulder and said in a subdued voice, "We've always felt this was such a beautiful piece."

His hand dropped and his shoulders sagged. "She treasured it."

It was a buckskin shirt and a war stick, a garment from one of those called "shirt wearers," and I knew immediately what it was, that it was more than just a shirt, it was part of the history I had always known. I felt my fingers go numb. From 1862? Isianti? Was this taken from one of those hanged at New Ulm after the Santee war with the U.S. for what is now Minnesota?

I had heard about the 1862 mass hanging of Isianti by the U.S. military all my life because my great-grandmother's relatives were implicated in the war led by Little Crow, the Mdewakantowan, the Wakpekuta, the Kaposas and Sissetons, and all the others.

My great-grandmother, they said, even knew the songs the warriors sang as they joined hands on the scaffold, and it was part of the family story that even when she was an old woman she could still sing some of those songs of courage. *Hoka-hey* kinds of songs that tell you that honorable Dakotahs do not fear death.

Immediately I knew sticks like this one were sacred. They were used almost exclusively by the Santees, and they were gathered from specific places and then rubbed and shaped and dyed with certain colors. I think others of our tribe use them in huge ceremonials now, like the Sun Dance, maybe. But these were different. There was only one stick folded in the buckskin shirt and it was striped red, which meant that the carrier had been to war in defense of the people.

Who had gathered the sticks from which this one came? Who had rubbed them and made the stripes by binding them with porcupine quills? How had this been saved from the same death met by its carrier? And why?

"We don't know where it came from," the husband was saying apologetically, as though reading my thoughts, "and so I can't give you much information."

"How did your wife's family come to have it?"

"I really don't know. We have had it appraised and it is worth thousands. I'll get the appraisal sheet for you from the other room."

I held the slender war stick in my hands and looked down at the treasure, knowing that I was looking at centuries of an unwritten history.

History.

When I was about four years old, afraid of the dark, running to Grandpa's bed crying, he gathered me up in his arms, and like he often did, he told me not to be afraid, and told me this story:

"This woman," he said, "she was your great-grandmother on the Tatiopa side of the family, a Yankton Indian woman who became known for her ability to tell the people what they needed to know in order to be strong.

"Once, this woman needed some special kind of wood, some sticks . . . and she deliberately sent a young man to go to a special place to do a dangerous thing, a hard thing," the old man said, rambling and hesitant as he often was when he recalled the stories, "and she was always like that because, you know, that's the way you raise boys."

He fidgeted.

"You know that?" he asked.

"Nope."

"Yeah. Boys are hard to raise, you know. That's what women always say."

He smiled and raised his eyebrows and nodded as though we had a secret.

A woman, they say, knew where a certain kind of wood grew in certain canyons and marshes, but when the young man went there to get them, he found the place littered with bones. He started to cut some limbs and saw that he was in a den of snakes that were striped red and white and black and they tried to bite him. He was afraid, but when he sang a song the old people had taught him, the snakes turned into cherry bushes and he gathered up some fragile and supple limbs and took them home to his grandmother. And she thanked him for the roots.

It's one of the ironies of life, I suppose, that someone like me who has never been very courageous and never much interested in religion, now because of the generosity or foolishness, whichever you wish to call it, of a drugged-out crazy white woman, I suddenly found myself in possession of a sacred shirt . . . a shirt made by one of the historical Isianti. And I possess one of the sticks that was carried into war by our relatives during a dangerous and difficult time.

As I ran my hand over the old buckskin, I felt the geometric designs of a snake head painted on the front shoulders along with a zigzag design of a lightning strike in colors that aren't used much anymore, the greasy yellow and the dark, dull purple. And red, the color of blood. The designs had smoothed edges and some of them were almost faded into a kind of ugly greenish brown—from age, I supposed.

As I felt the geometric designs of a snake head and the zigzag design of lightning I wondered: Whose shirt is this? Who used this shirt and for what purpose? And how did the family of the white woman addicted to drugs come to possess it? Why did it have a snake on it?

Zu-zu-e-cha . . . he really likes to come out after the sun goes down and listen to the stories the Dakotahs tell, and so in the summertime, certain stories are never told after dark. Although I really never watched out for snakes and didn't know much about their relationship to humans when I was growing up on the reservation, I was always cautioned to be careful around the poisonous ones . . . I was told that they would listen to humans, but other than that I knew very little about their long history as primordial creatures. The presence of the snake on the shirt wearer's garment was a puzzle to me.

As a kid, I would sometimes walk down a path crowded with tall weeds, catching a glimpse of web-like snake skins recently shed. In August, usually. A time when rattlers are blind and deaf and they strike out at anything. It must be a terrible time for them, to shrug off the old and be re-created. It was something I had never watched, but I've always wanted to. But I am unaware of how it really happens. Does it take a long time? Hours? Minutes? Days? Do they suffer?

Sometimes I would pick up the skins and examine them more closely, and it always made me shiver because I knew they had at one time been living things, and now what was left were long, fragile pieces of crinkled parchment that could be blown away in the slightest breeze. The live ones never appeared dangerous to me, and when I would see them lying stretched out on a rock in the sun in the fall of the year just before they went to their dens along the river, they would just look like brown ropes, even though I could make out the diamonds on the back. Even coiled, tongue licking and rattles shaking, they seemed pitiful.

One time on my way to the chicken house, I watched a rattlesnake stretched out on the slope eating an egg. He was gorged and swollen and you could see his cream-colored belly bulged out on each side. I was surprised at how big his mouth was, a kind of square opening, white inside with yellow yolk and pieces of shell unaccountably smeared, and I watched, in fascination, the snake's beady eyes almost disappearing into the designs of the scaly yet smooth rectangular head. He was totally inert and helpless.

In spite of all the things I had been told, I didn't know I wasn't supposed to watch a snake eating. I didn't know that until later when I told my grandfather about what I had seen and he said I would have to go to old Grass Rope and discuss it with him and tell him that it had happened, because he said I was never to watch such a thing.

I didn't go to see the old spiritual man like my grandfather had advised. I don't know why. Now, years later, I can't help feeling disappointed in myself.

The design on the buckskin shirt was graceful, but the smell from the garment was unforgettable. Something like rotting grass, maybe, but at the same time it was clean like the prairie grass just after a rain. Stars were clustered above and below the snake design, and like the quick white flames of a morning sunrise, they seemed to contract and deepen and then disappear and then return. I probably should have known even then there was something about the snake that was noteworthy and that each one has its own spirit, its own particular sound and songs that people can never hear.

I've never known anything about the legends, but I do know that these matters are often ritualized by the people. Once I saw the old man cut a long slash in the ground to symbolize the bed of a snake, and even though my remembrance is quite dim, I think it was for the commemoration of a death among his wife's Santee and Yankton relatives. No one told me, but I guessed the snake spirit was represented by each root used in some of the ceremonies of the Santee and Yankton relatives of my grandmother. It was a ritual meant to help humans understand, especially those who are grieving about death, that all worlds are related.

I looked down at the shirt. The husband of the woman who had willed this gift to me moved close again, and I moved away again. He touched my shoulder and said in a subdued voice, "Isn't it beautiful?"

I hardly heard what he was saying because the snake design and the odor coming from the folds of the shirt overwhelmed me. The wet root smell reminded me that in his ceremonies, the old man would bundle up the roots and use them to throw water on the rocks as he prepared sweatlodge and then put them back in the water, and I often saw him handle them very carefully and slowly. The smell was very familiar. I was astounded to think that this odor had made its way into the modern world from a hundred years in the past. This was a very special gift and I had no illusions that I was in any way deserving.

The ways to mediate the snake spirits were not ways that I had ever paid attention to, but now I was shocked at the connection I felt between this gift shirt with the snake design and the ceremonial actions of the old man.

He handled water and roots that memorable time when old Chekpa's wife died and it was said she was lingering near even after they had buried her in the mixed traditional-modern way that was practiced at that time. It seemed like she did not want to go to the next world and she had to have some special honoring to be enticed to leave the earth.

Maybe snakes are like that, too, I thought. Maybe when I touched their parchment skins abandoned in a rebirth I felt a kinship because they, too, had come to love the earth.

"Dakotahs learn to love the earth and often they hesitate after death," was the old man's prayer, and I heard him sing many songs at that time, but I never knew them and hardly remembered them even as I looked down at the aged shirt. I heard only a faint, dull sound in my ears like a train in the distance or the sound of a ferry crossing a body of water miles away.

The roots seemed important at those times when my grandfather tried to ease the pain of death in our community. Even I noticed that as they were bundled in a certain way, and as the water on the stones was meant to purify, to take away all worldly life, there was a sorrow explained in our language which can be translated as "They don't want to leave," and there was on his part a clear insight into the fundamental mysteries of life.

Though my grandfather was just an old man like any other, he knew many things, and I was anxious to show him the gift and ask him: Was the man who owned this shirt *wakicun*? Was the owner of it one of the people in whom the original tribal government was vested, the government of the Dakotapi? Was he one of those appointed by the old men? It was important to know that because if that was so, the hanging of the men by the U.S. military in Minnesota was a political matter that has rarely been understood. I'm always interested in the politics of any situation. If the truth were known, I have always been more interested in the political matters than in the cultural or religious matters of my people. I hate to admit it, and often I don't.

If the shirt was what I was now thinking it was, the hanging of the men could take on very different meaning. It was not about criminal behavior. It was not about fate or destiny. Not even revenge, and for sure, not an accident of history. Instead, it was a cruel strategy by Americans to conquer the Dakota people any way they could. It was a means to take away their power no matter what crime had to be undertaken against them. The hanging, then, was not about law. Instead, it was about raw power of one people over another.

If the shirt was from *wakicun*, I was thinking, it seemed clear to me that the mass hanging was something more than mere legal punishment or historical fact. It meant that these tribal men were powerful and honorable men defending their homelands as many patriots throughout history have done; therefore, they had to be destroyed.

It meant they could not be allowed to live to lead the people out of their terrible prostrations. From the time of the ancestors, these were men who were nationalists and therefore dangerous to those intent upon colonization.

I wasn't sure that the old man would want to talk to me about this kind of political reality; nonetheless I couldn't wait to take the bundle to him. Even before I left the husband's presence, and even before I talked to the old man, I understood now that this shirt had very likely belonged to a Dakotah leader who was deeply attached to our heritage and, therefore, our future.

In spite of how grateful I felt to the husband and that miserable woman who was his wife for giving the stolen artifact back into Indian hands, I still hated the notion of what had happened, and my questions could be seen as intrusive and rude.

How did the woman's family get this stuff? Probably no one took these things from the grave of the shirt owner, because it is a fact of history that these Sioux warriors were held prisoner at Fort Snelling for many days and weeks and years before they were taken to the hanging place, which means that the deceased probably wasn't wearing the shirt at the time of his death. I say "probably" because no one can really know for sure and all the witnesses themselves are dead.

Was the man carrying it in his bundles and did the military men divest him of it as he walked to his death? Did the military or the other pioneer folks in the community go into the Indian homes and ransack them after the hanging, or did the shirt wearer give it to someone in the tribal community for safekeeping only to be betrayed? Was he *wa-ki-con-za* and, if he was, were there others to whom he would have given his shirt?

Perhaps it was stolen by one of the white woman's relatives or someone who worked for the U.S. military. It is said in various historical writings that it was a common practice for U.S. soldiers to morbidly loot Indian battlefields, the death scenes, the villages where people lived. It may be crude to say, but don't you suppose that much of the stuff of museums comes from unsavory places and actions? Maybe some desperate Santee person sold it to traders for food during the terrible period of starvation which followed the entire calamity. In the presence of the shirt, these questions raced through my mind, reflecting what I imagined were the chaotic events of war. As I touched the sacred garment I recognized that while it told much of the story of the Little Crow War of the Santees, it kept its own secrets of that time that could, perhaps, never be known. My questions, though, even if they can never be answered, must be asked by someone.

The sides of the hide shirt were long in front and back, like the leg part of the deer. The fringes seemed very long. The striped stick was wrapped in buckskin and hung from the front of the shirt where the pouch was also hanging. I noticed that there was no black striped stick, which could mean that the shirt wearer might have been inexperienced in killing—young, perhaps, because it is believed that the black stick was used only if he had killed an enemy.

Yet, he kept a pouch, which might have been a clue to the fact that he was not young, because these pouches were usually carried by mature men. Maybe these items had been looted from several warriors, not just one; some of them, perhaps, had more experience and more significant leadership roles than others. Who were they? Who was this shirt wearer? Could we ever know?

It's known that only *wakicun* and their superiors carried these long, ornamental pipe bags for which the Dakotas were noted. Nowadays, in the modern world everyone carries them, even women and white people, and you see them carried by the traditional dancers at powwows; but in the old days seeing a pouch like this one was a rare thing. Sitting Bull of the Hunkpati and American Horse of the Oglalas were known to be carriers of these special pouches.

My grandmother said that Little Crow and his lieutenants carried them, even though the white histories I've read have been anxious to condemn these Santee Mdewakantowan and Wahpekute chieftains as savage people who did not have the good will of the tribal people. My grandmother insisted that those who carried these pouches understood the virtue of *wa-ki-ci-un-yan* (to offer sacrifice) and it meant a lot to the community.

I had always been told, too, that these long-fringed, hair-fringed shirts were said to be "owned by the tribe," not by individuals, and this made it even more puzzling as to how the drug addict's family had come to possess it. These were very special things that were kept by very special people who had the general welfare and safety and protection of the tribe and good hunting and healthful campsites as their business and as their duties. These things hadn't been gotten from just anybody.

I shook hands with the husband and thanked him and took the precious wrapped bundle and put it in the trunk of the Limo. I slammed the trunk lid, hooked it down with a bungee cord, and drove off in a haze of confusion, carefully counting the aspens as I drove down the private lane. Six. Seven. Eight. In my rearview mirror I caught a glimpse of the husband watching with sadness etched in his battered face. I wondered if I'd see him again.

When I got home I put the bundle under my bed and fell immediately into an untroubled but brief sleep thinking briefly about how ironic it was that the clothes of my great-grandmother's deceased relative were now worth thousands of dollars on the "museum" market, to say nothing of the "collector's world."

In the night I woke and lay there trying to come to some understanding of recent events, uneasy now and confused. These people who had this shirt for a hundred years or more were "collectors," I assumed now. Since I had never been in a real museum, like the Smithsonian, or even the Institute in Minneapolis, I had little insight into all of this, but I knew enough to know that to be a "collector" of Indian possessions could hardly be considered an honorable occupation. My mixed feelings about the husband and his strange wife persisted.

As I tossed and turned until dawn, I struggled with thoughts about the cultural meaning of the beautiful shirt and the intention of the artisan who made it. What was the meaning of the snake? And the stars? What about the red stick? Who has earned the right to possess it now in the modern world? Not the husband and his awful wife, for sure! And, for sure, not me, a guy with pathetically shallow insights whose life is an everyday gamble.

I went to work at the hospital the next day still troubled by all of this, but I tried to act unconcerned.

Accidents are just accidents, after all.

CHAPTER 11

To make my day, Dorothy showed up again on Saturday. I decided that maybe the stars were in the right places after all, and I was nothing if not thankful because I was in real bad shape thinking of all the tasks left to me that seemed to be of overwhelming importance.

"What are you going to do with the shirt?" she asked as she stood at the stove heating up some coffee.

"I don't know."

I put on a tape. It was George Jones and Tammy Wynette and they were singing, "We're gonna ho-o-o-o-ld on . . ."

I turned and said sarcastically, "Tears your heart out, huh?"

"Yeah," she responded, indignant about my sour attitude, but smiling.

I put my arms around her and sighed, a signal of my rugged frame of mind. "You know, I've never understood the obsession for country's sentimental shit."

"I like it," she said.

Crap, I thought, but I said nothing.

Yeah, hold on.

She was quiet in my arms.

My thoughts were not about romance but about war crimes and those who get away with it, those who were never tried or executed, but who went about their lives as innocents; the others who held on, those who died at the hands of war criminals or were released or hanged, all seemingly at the whimsy of a mean but relentless history.

Yeah, I thought about Tony's suicide, the holding on.

Restless and feeling my anger, Dorothy got up for a moment, took a look out the dark window, and said, "It's going to rain."

Turning, she smiled, and I put my hands on her waist and drew her to me. She was warm and soft and I closed my eyes and kissed her, and suddenly I knew that I could tell her anything.

As she lay beside me, I told her about my Uncle Tony shooting himself, and she said she'd often had thoughts about death but never about suicide because suicide requires, she said, an urge that is irresistible and she never had that compulsion. I felt better about Tony when she said that.

Then, to make light of it, she said, "Besides, I don't like pain. I'm such a coward . . ."

We smiled at that.

"Maybe shooting yourself, you don't have any pain."

"Yeah? Maybe. Suicide would be better than Allie's death," she said. "It must have been unbearable."

"It's better than breaking your neck in a public hanging, too," I said, letting the irony show in my voice.

There was a long pause when neither of us could speak. Trying to be casual about this conversation wasn't working for either of us.

"Death is a sacred thing," I said finally, not thinking so much about Allie, not even about Uncle Tony, but thinking about the Santee patriots over a hundred years ago in Minnesota, hanging by their necks from the bare scaffold, and how, in preparation, they had joined hands, and how they sang with each other and to each other on the scaffold and to all the thousands of witnesses, mostly white, who had gathered there in a frenzy of hatred and revenge.

Thousands of white witnesses, they say, gathered to see the largest mass hanging in the history of this country, only they didn't know it then, that what they were seeing would go down in history as the only mass hanging ever in this country.

Instead, they were probably there out of curiosity, and also because they saw themselves as victims of a people they considered savages. The witnesses were, after all, participants of a new society, immigrants in a new country, and Indians were the outsiders, to them, unassimilable and dangerous. Revenge had a lot to do with that event, and the truth is killing as remedy has always been a virtue in some societies. Getting rid of a degenerate element is the motive of colonists. Some historians have said that as many as ten thousand people from all over the region came to watch the hanging.

As the Dakotahs sang, their hearts must have been full yet desolate, livid yet numbed from war and humiliation and hunger, and still they sang songs of courage and *wiconi* and the beautiful *maka*.

Just before I turned out the light I said, "Sacred is how it is that the Santees think of death. It's not just sad. It is a holy thing. That's why they make art of it. You know, ceremony, ritual."

"Yes," she said. Half asleep and half awake, we talked into the night and I told her about how the horses had danced at old Grey Iron's funeral. Had I told her this before? Was I telling it again?

"It wasn't sad," I said. "It was like a ceremony."

"The truth is, Phil," Dorothy told me in her realistic, down-to-earth voice, "some people survive and some people don't."

"Is it really that simple?"

"I think so."

I touched her face, her nose, lips, cheekbones, and felt the warmth between her thighs. She had attitude and I liked her a lot. Should I tell her how much I liked her? Tell her that she was so beautiful? To make light of a suddenly intimate moment I said, "Hey, I like the way you look . . . you are so pretty . . . you know that, don't you?"

I could feel her smiling in the dark.

"But, even when you're old . . . even when your teeth all fall out, hey, I'll still love you, babe . . ."

She had no answer for that and I wondered why. What was she thinking?

After a brief and uncomfortable silence when she paid no attention to my words, dismissing them as either unimportant or foolish, she began tentatively, "When your Uncle Tony . . . uh . . . did himself in, you told yourself it was okay, didn't you?"

I didn't answer.

"Didn't you?"

"Yeah. I suppose."

"That he had the right to take his own life?"

"Uh-huh."

"That's what we do, you know, as people who don't know what else to do with our grief. But what most people really should say and what they really should believe is that he is just one of those who would not . . . could not . . . survive it. And, we'll never know why . . ."

Her voice trailed off as though she was asking a question.

For just a moment I felt a stab of anger, but just as quickly my resistance to that idea receded and was replaced by a moving torrent of emotion. As I lay still beside her I saw the black river rising, and it turned red, and there was the blood and Clarissa's mournful weeping and that awful scene of Tony's grisly death. I turned and put my arms around Dorothy and wept like a child. Her breasts were pressed hard against me and her back was warm and damp.

"*Cheya sni ye,*" she said over and over, yet she cried with me.

I would remember that night as the first and last time I cried for my Uncle Tony.

"The truth is"—I would remember her words forever—"some people survive and some don't and we may never know why."

That may not sound profound to some people, but for me, it was the first sensible thing I'd heard in answer to profoundly disturbing events.

Allie couldn't survive his life. The white woman drug addict couldn't survive her life. Neither could my Uncle Tony. Neither could the Isianti patriots at the hanging scaffold in New Ulm. And now they all had become history. More devastating than death itself, few had made tribal art of their deaths, and that's why we survivors continue to take the blame and feel responsible.

It was clear to me now as I turned over and stared into the dark ceiling that it was a matter of Survival, not Death. I knew then that Dorothy and I were among the survivors. It was clear then that I had been drifting in my own sorrow, "by accident" going about my so-called life emptying bedpans and changing sheets for people I didn't know, and I was doing it because I couldn't make sense of senseless death. And because I wanted an explanation for things that had no explanations. I remembered how my Auntie Aurelia had often said, "Some things just are, Philip."

I had thought that Uncle Tony's suicide was about Death. Now I find that I'm willing . . . no, needing . . . to believe in a woman whose spirit could see some feeble hint of light in the darkness we live in, a woman telling me things I've always known, her face not having lost that childish look, yet expressing a kind of womanly arrogance, convincing me that there is a new way to look at old ideas—and that Tony's awful death is about Survival.

"In the Indian world," said Dorothy in her soft voice, "we are surrounded by a world of dead people, our ancestors, the *wanagi*, the people who have gone to the other side, and that's all right, Phil, it's all right . . ."

She looked at me like she could see right through me. As she talked I felt I could catch a glimpse of that spirit myself.

". . . and I am really comforted about that." Her eyes shone.

"You are?"

"Yes," she said with much emphasis. "Otherwise, if I didn't know that and if I didn't care, I couldn't bear it. Really, Phil. I could never stand it. I'd be like my mother, who hasn't gotten out of her bed since Allie's death."

I had never put things into the perspective of Dorothy's plain logic: some people survive, some don't. And what I made of Dorothy's talking into the night was this: *there are probably no accidents.*

CHAPTER 12

At Big Pipe's place, the bundle with the warrior shirt was placed on the table, and I thought the old man would open the bundle and look at the shirt right away. Instead he prepared the ritual smudging and then went outside to start the fire for heating the stones.

As I watched his bent, frail body and his shaking hands on the wobbling cane, I felt a moment of real despair. I thought how disappointing it must have been to him that one son simply disappeared and another, my Uncle Anthony, had been a man who understood nothing of the gift of life the old man had given him.

On the one hand, Tony grew up and could have been in touch with the complexity of a good life had he wanted to, but then he went to school and then he went to the Army and in either case, he remained unable to say anything about what was inside of him. After the Army, time stops for Uncle Tony and he comes home, is pulled into cautious movements by the police and others, spends his time in bars, and, too soon, lies in his coffin, all in the space of a few short years.

The three of us, Tony and me and the old man, and sometimes Uncle Jason, spent a lot of our time fishing. Tony could never think of himself getting old, and I couldn't think of him that way, either. Sometimes my Uncle Sheridan went with us, but most often he begged off for one reason or another, and when he disappeared we hardly knew he was gone. So we climbed the hills and hunted grouse and deer, most of the time in what I took then to be a convivial silence but now recognize as an agonizing fear—a curious need to be close to another human being, but an unrelieved need, also, for isolation.

It is a conflict we've struggled with, and only now do I know what it meant that we tried so hard to bring us together in a male relationship closer than brothers and sisters. When he was drunk, Uncle Tony would want to talk to me, but he never made much sense and often I didn't listen. I didn't even listen. The last time I didn't even listen. And then I saw his bloody death.

Watching the old man prepare the fire, I put Uncle Tony out of my thoughts and I stood staring into the chilly gloom overlooking the dull river, waiting for the fire to get the stones white hot and the embers reddened like the flash of the sun. By mere chance I noticed a spider in its web in the corner of the porch eaves. It was shaking in the wind, back and forth, back and forth. The spider held on grudgingly and curled into a brown ball when it started to rain.

The fields were wet and the river, dark rimmed by stark, bare trees in the distance, was shrouded in low clouds and fog. It rained all weekend but we refused to put off everything. We went ahead. I walked a mile up the gravel road while I waited and retrieved the old man's mail from his mailbox. Dead leaves were clinging to my boots and I scraped them off as I walked.

I thought I heard something behind me and turned a couple of times, but there was nothing there, not even the little sparrows that ordinarily hang in the air. I knew I should've been more attentive to the sacred process of honoring the spirits of the dead, as the old man was, but as usual I was restless and I felt this whole thing was real time-consuming.

As a nonbeliever I just didn't want to get too involved. I looked up at the sky with its gray, wet omens hovering over the land, and felt the impatience of the persistent, strong wind always blowing along the Missouri River, and knew that it wouldn't be put off much longer. These were signals that would make everything biting cold real soon. There is nothing like that river cold, the bare trees against the sky; there is no place as primal as the places where the huge boulders lie along this shore.

We kept the fire going and went into the sweat lodge for purification about midday. It seemed pitiful that it was only my grandfather and me who were making the ceremony for the bundle of holy things. Usually, the old man remarked, this is a communal thing. In my own thinking, it seemed more to be a reflection of hard times than outright abuse or neglect by the people.

"The *Ikce* will be here," the old man assured me, "and the spirit world will be okay with what we are doing."

It was only after the hours of preparation and the washing of the harmful things from our bodies and from the lodge that we viewed the gift from the white woman and her husband. The old man said very little but was visibly moved and he wept. Almost immediately, he began considering this return an effective remedy for the fractured history of the tribe.

"It is not ours," I said, thinking what he was thinking. "It is not mine."

"You are right, we must also now do another return gesture, be sure that it gets to its rightful owners, the *wakicun*," he said. "You must make arrangements."

I didn't know how to go about doing that, but I knew that I'd better find out. In the meantime, the bundle would be in the care of my grandfather.

I didn't make it back to town for two days, missing work at the hospital for the first time. After driving the Limo as fast as the speed limit would allow from the places where I hung out, the cold air all around, I'd felt exhausted and looked forward to getting to work, if for no other reason than to warm up.

The chill was becoming unbearable even for late autumn, and it was a relief to walk through the heavy doors of the hospital, the swish of the warm air in my face from the doors as they swung slowly shut, the vacuum apparatus of the automatic doors causing air to rush toward the outside. I made my excuses to Sister and told her that we have no telephone service at my grandfather's place so I couldn't notify them of my absence, and that I had urgent family business and I was sorry.

Sister Amabolis said it was okay and I'd better get to work. My jacket, stiff as ice, suddenly felt warm and I was energized. The routine at the hospital was getting easier for me now that I knew my way around, but I felt more than ever now that it was only a question of time before I'd leave.

Robert didn't eat in the cafeteria any more, but Claire did. Now, since this episode of Allie Eagle's death and the talk about my being given a gift by Mrs. Larson, Claire seemed to think we had something in common, so every time she saw me, especially when she saw me in the cafeteria, she'd make it her business to come over and sit down and in her own white-girl way engage me in conversation—most of it pretty trivial, I thought.

The first time this happened it was really an odd sort of conversation and I think we both realized how uncomfortable we were with one another.

"Do you have folks, Philip? Your mother and dad?"

"Sure."

"Oh, yes?" Cheerful, bright. "Where do they live?"

Jeez, I hate perky, I thought.

"Oh, they live out on the rez."

"Um-mm," and she lowered her head, kind of like she was embarrassed. They could be on the moon for all she knew about the reservation.

"So, you live alone?"

When I didn't answer she kept right on with the questions. "Here then, in town, huh?"

"Yeah. Mostly."

"Do you go out, uh, out there, home . . . quite often then?"

"Yeah. Sometimes."

"What're you going to do with the buckskin shirt?"

"I don't know."

"Do you think it's sacred?"

"Uh-huh."

"What does that mean? Could you explain it to me?"

"Well, no, I can't really explain it."

"Well, then, how do you know it's sacred?"

"Oh, it's hard to explain."

"I really would like to know, Philip. I'm interested in that kind of thing."

"What kind of thing?"

"Oh, you know . . . Indian spirituality."

"Oh."

I grabbed up my tray and headed over to the stand to place it where they would pick it up for the dishwasher. "I gotta go," I said hurriedly. I know Claire thought I was rude, or maybe she thought she was, because the next time I saw her in the cafeteria, she came over and apologized.

"I didn't mean to be nosy."

"No. No. That's okay."

"Say, would you like to come over to my place for supper sometime?"

"Oh. Yeah. Sure."

"When? Can you come this Saturday?"

"Well, maybe some other time. I can't make it Saturday."

"Yes, well . . ."

"Um . . . some other time, maybe."

It was the last thing I wanted to do, but I wanted to be polite so I hedged a little bit. To go to her place and try out some more of the kind of conversation we were having didn't appeal to me. It seemed clear that I wasn't too interested in her or her life or anything about her, and I figured she was just interested in me because I was Indian. Something different from her usual friends. Exotic, huh? Spiritual?

I remembered seeing that movie *Guess Who's Coming to Dinner*, with Sidney Poitier. Some white girl brings home this black guy, and Spencer Tracy just about goes postal but tries in his own reasonable way to be reasonable. Maybe it was the first "politically correct" movie and it was a big hit.

I couldn't see my grandpa sitting around trying to answer this Claire chick's questions. Nope, I thought, the old man's no Spencer Tracy.

"She's a nice person," I told Dorothy later, "but, you know. Just not my type."

"Yeah?" She raised her eyebrows. "What's your type?"

I shrugged.

"Am I your type?"

"Sure." I grabbed her and kissed her. We fumbled around and bumped into the furniture and laughed. She looked at me hard for several long moments and as she did I knew my casual "sure" was something more than just an offhand admission. It was something I might desert everything for.

"You know, in the Indian way you shouldn't have too much to do with white people. White women, in particular."

"Yeah. I know." I smiled and said, "Look, my mom told me about all this . . . never to speak to strangers . . . I know . . ." That set her off and she laughed and took my arm.

"Let me tell you a story," she began. "It's a story about myself—"

Abruptly, I put my hand on hers, wanting to be near but wanting, too, to keep everything light.

"Say, you're not going to confess, are you?"

She laughed nervously. "Yeah? Well, maybe . . . but anyway, you know when I was in Bismarck I really had a tough time, speaking of having to do with strangers. I guess you know that I married a stranger."

"No. I didn't know that."

"Well, not exactly a stranger. He was Winnebago, from Nebraska."

"Oh."

After a brief pause I raised my eyebrows and said, "Well, yeah, that's strange, all right," and we both laughed thinking about all the jokes between the Winnebagos and the Siouxs.

"How come you left him?"

"Oh. It's a long story, but in a nutshell, he just didn't help me."

"Help you what?"

"Anything." She flung the word at me as though I should know without having to ask dumb questions.

"Besides," she said, looking at me with clear, dark eyes, "I want a man who can talk to me in our language . . . sometimes."

"Yeah?"

"Yeah." She shrugged and sighed as though she couldn't explain. "Do you understand that?"

"Sure, I do."

"Albert's dad, he's a good person. I just don't want him the way . . ." She didn't finish. "You know, I want a guy who loves me and who can talk to me in our language . . . in Dakotah. I don't know . . ." Her voice trailed off.

"Like me?"

She just looked at me.

Maybe I was being too hopeful. Not that I know that much about women, but I immediately thought that nothing turns them off more than a guy who is too available. Maybe I ought to try to be hard to get.

Too late, Pipe, I thought, too goddamned late!

"Well, let me tell you about this thing . . ."

I put my head back and felt the tension in my shoulders.

"You want to hear this or not?"

"Yeah. I want to hear it."

"One time at Albert's school I was called to the school office and was confronted by a North Dakota social worker about how many times he had missed school, and was told that I was being investigated and would be reported for child abuse and neglect."

"Jeez . . . that's pretty threatening, isn't it?"

"Well, yeah. I was really scared."

"And, so . . ."

"And so . . . well, he had missed a lot of school. I don't argue about that! We'd had a lot of car trouble. And, listen, Albert's dad . . . he couldn't fix nothing!

I'm used to the guys in my family who can keep any old jalopy on the road . . . you know, they always got their heads under the hood of some old junker! But, anyway, it was icy in the wintertime and sometimes the car wouldn't start, and one time we had a fender bender and then Albert got chicken pox and all kinds of shit happened . . ."

She paused for dramatic effect.

"It turned out that social worker had been watching us ever since we moved into that town. She had a bead on us right from the beginning."

"How do you know that?"

"After I got home from work that night, after the meeting with the school people and the social worker . . . she never even took off her coat during the whole time she was bawling me out and threatening me right there in front of my kid. Well, after that . . . Albert told me that he knew her, and when I asked him how he knew her he said one time, one weekend day, he said, she had driven her car up to the curb where he was playing with his cousin at the neighborhood church playground and asked him a whole bunch of questions."

"What kind of questions?"

"Questions like 'where is your father?' and 'why don't you live on the reservation?' and 'what does your father do?' and 'how long have you lived here?' and 'where did you move here from?' Stuff like that."

"She was watching you?"

"Yeah. *They* were watching us. You know, the social services people and the so-called child protection people. I found out later they do that with every Indian family that moves into town—and particularly with single mothers—all the time."

"That's pretty scary, all right."

"It's one of the reasons I moved home."

"You quit school?"

"Yeah. I left. And I came home."

"Do you think it made an impression on Albert?"

"Well, yeah. I think he worries about whether or not I can take care of him . . . and us. It has made him doubt me."

"Is it confusing that Albert doesn't live with his dad?"

"Yeah. I think it is."

"Do you talk to him about it?"

"No, not really. Not unless he asks."

"Does he ask?"

"No. I mean, hardly ever. It seems all right with him, so we just never bring up the subject."

"Why don't you talk to him?"

"About his dad?"

"Yes."

"Nope. I'm just not going to go there. I'm not," she said emphatically.

Then, like she was reading my thoughts, she said, "I wish he would stay small forever."

I wondered if it was "all right" with Albert, like it had been "all right" with me when my mom kicked my dad out. But, I said nothing more. If there is something I don't know anything about, it is the relationship between a mother and her son.

CHAPTER 13

The scaffold seemed grand and at the same time flimsy in the prairie landscape. The wind, sharp and clean, seemed to me to have come from the first world when the stars were the only Dakotahs. To me, the whole thing was awesome and I couldn't believe what was happening. The gift. So strange and unexpected.

Now, the giving back.

The scaffold was made out of new wood and we had spent days peeling the small, supple trees, much like the people peel the tipi poles that are used for them to gather at the Sun Dance. Drawn like fireflies to the light, our Dakotah relatives came from everywhere as soon as they heard about the ceremony, from as far away as Canada and Niobrara and Minnesota, and as near as Crow Creek. Dorothy came with her parents to help, and they, like everyone, brought their own sharp scrapers for peeling, their sweetgrass and blankets and their memories.

Careful preparation made this a stage for a most significant drama about death and survival, and we felt good that we had prepared a foundation for the ways that the people always had for remembering and mourning and healing. It made up for a lot of neglect and isolation and grief that everyone felt. We knew we weren't alone.

It was cold and we dressed in warm coats, and Albert stood around and watched. When I saw him standing around, not exactly aimless, but not exactly engaged either, I was reminded of some days of my own childhood and felt happier than I'd felt in a long time. After the scaffold was finished, the men from the community came and put up a delicate-looking black wrought-iron fence around the holy place.

People from the communities came, making their way from what we now call the diaspora, and they shook hands with the old man and asked no questions. We stayed there inside the fence with the bundle for four days, first my grandpa and my Uncle Jason and then all of us.

My Auntie Aurelia was there, and in her bare feet she helped the other women bear the sacred object to its resting place beside the bones of the only three Santees who were identified several years ago and repatriated to the homelands. We did it for all of us, for ourselves and for the other relatives who are still lost, indefinable, and cannot be "kept" in the sacred way. The women struck the tree in the middle of the arbor with eagle-feather fans and sang songs that had not been heard for a hundred years. And we wept.

We didn't feel pitiful, but perhaps others who might have seen us thought of us that way, dozens of people standing with their prayers stuck in their throats, overlooking the gray, raging river and homelands of the *unktechis*, a dark and muddy river now swollen with the fall rains and early snow and its thawing sounds, noisy as a raspy animal in heat.

Who were we? The few scraggly survivors praying and talking and sharing thoughts, sustaining ourselves through a ceremony as old as the hills, holding hands with one another and telling stories and singing the songs of courage. Who were we and who had we become?

"My grandmother ran from the American soldiers," old Tilda Red Hail told us. "She ran for miles with two children, one carried on her back and the other trotting 'longside of her like a scared puppy. They finally made it across into Canada, but nobody ever saw them again alive, and only the tales of her bravery survived and made it back to the people."

"When my father's parents first came to the Crow Creek compound," Dorothy said, "there were fifty-foot-high fences around the agency, and Indians outside of that could be shot on sight, no questions asked."

Her mother added quietly: "We heard they got $200 for every dead Indian they brought in."

"In truth, those Indian survivors who must have felt old even before they were old, they told us how to live our lives as Dakotahs," said Daryl Saul, a relative who had come here from Niobrara for the spirit ceremony, "those people who felt old even before they were old."

He wept and sang. As his song was lifted into the air, I heard the rushing sound of hundreds of birds in flight over my right shoulder, and I looked into the suddenly brightened sky, startled, and they flashed silver in the sun and swooped over us and then vanished. We stood stunned and the sun blazed, warm on our shoulders.

The long four days of restoration ended. They were the longest days of my life.

Just after the ceremony was ended and everyone was packing up getting ready to leave, I watched as Auntie Aurelia's new man, Hermist, helped her carry her belongings to a car parked out in the makeshift parking lot beside the road. She settled herself in the front seat and he arranged a blanket over her knees.

As they drove away, she stared at me from the window knowing that there was nothing in our lives that could begin or end arbitrarily. I wondered if she was thinking that there is an unstoppable path that one must follow toward someplace or something and it is a path that we cannot see or determine. Thinking about that, I wondered what it meant to my "accidental" life. I lifted my hand in gratitude as the car moved from the gathering.

Dorothy and I sat on a bench in the cold air, and she told me she was going to return to her husband.

I could say nothing for several long minutes. Motionless, we watched the people leave.

"Why would you go back now, especially after this?" I gestured toward the mound.

She gathered her coat around her and shrugged.

"I don't know. It's just the right thing to do, I think."

"Why would you go back to a man who didn't 'help you'?" I asked her, still thinking of Aurelia's departing look, a look neither weak nor frightened nor defeated, a look too blurred and rapidly glimpsed, but one which I would remember as both indistinct and steady.

"Because he wants me to come back."

"What kind of reason is that?"

She looked at me and then down at the trampled leaves. She leaned her elbow on the wooden table and rubbed her forehead like it hurt or like it was a source of tension.

She was silent and I felt awful, spouting one question after another. Why are you doing this? What about us? Don't you love me? All the arrogant questions posed by all the fools in love you've ever known.

I know I'm not being very original, but I felt like I'd just been kicked in the stomach. I guess I should have known there was more to this than I had first thought when I saw her unexpectedly hurrying up the steps of the hospital that bad day of her brother's death. Women, perhaps, have unfathomable obligations.

"What about us?" I asked again, and my question hung in the air and we couldn't move on. I felt myself being selfish and mean, but also alone, immensely alone; not since I saw Tony die on the cluttered floor of his trailer house had I felt so alone.

Finally, she said: "Is this going to turn into a big fight?"

"No. I don't want to fight with you. I just want to know . . . uh . . . why. That's all . . . why? Why, Dorothy?"

"You always want to know why."

"Yeah . . . well, why?"

"Because he wants me to come back."

I had a notion to say, "But, that's dumb. That is just profoundly dumb, Dorothy." But, I didn't say it.

Instead I asked, "What do you want?," emphasizing the word "you."

She opened her mouth to speak but then shrugged.

"I'm confused, Dorothy."

Her eyes met mine for just a moment.

"You don't seem like the kind of woman who, like so many others, is living for somebody else . . . unable to do what you want. You aren't like me, struggling to get along with Clarissa and paying attention to what the old man thinks and . . . always trying to—"

"Oh yeah. I am!" she interrupted.

"No . . . you're not! You're not a woman who believes in some kind of penitential service. You're no nun, Dorothy."

"No, maybe not," she said, ". . . but you've got to understand, Philip."

"Yeah . . . I'm trying . . ."

"I've got Albert."

That stopped me.

"What I mean is, Philip, *we've* got Albert. His dad and me. Albert's dad is a good person and he loves us."

She was in tears.

"Don't you see, Philip?"

After that there was not much to say, so I said the only thing I could think of: "But, he can't talk to you in Indian."

I took her hand in mine and held it for a long time.

"I know," she whispered at last.

I wanted to put my arms around her but I didn't. After all, she was raised among Dakotahs. And so was I. What could we expect?

As we walked away with my grandfather, he said to me, "Now you can go there to that spot overlooking the river anytime, and you can see nothing there except the river and the dried leaves, and you can feel nothing touching your face or your arms except the wind. You can pray there and be yourself and know that the grinning spirits have conducted their own ceremonies in the heavens to match the doings of mere humans, and that they will love us."

We walked on, hearing only the crunching of our footsteps on the hard earth.

"It's the best place on earth," he said, looking back. "And I thank you, my grandson."

It was more gratitude than I deserved because I had done nothing to find out how the white hospital woman, the pitiful, drug-addicted woman, had come to possess the sacred objects in the first place, and until I knew that, the story would be unfinished.

As we drove away from the circle where the community had gathered, I selfishly could think of nothing but my own misery. Dorothy and her son, who in his childlike wisdom knew that everything had changed, sat in stony silence on the drive back to her parents' place. When we got there, I sat behind the wheel while she and the little boy gathered their things from the Limo and went inside the house.

I turned the car around in the driveway and slowly drove away, feeling sadder than I'd ever felt in my life. I have not spoken to them since.

CHAPTER 14

The Church board of inquiry was meeting just a few blocks from the hospital. It was weeks after the repatriation of the artifacts, and it seemed like forever since I had said my last words to Dorothy, who was forever on my mind. I worked some on the night shift and slept during the day. Sometimes I volunteered for overtime. To be what I'm not and never have been seemed my lot. But I could think of little that mattered to me personally. I seemed to surround myself with people who would try to make me into something I never would have been. Talkative. Grinning. It was so depressing that it made me try to put my head down and never want to look up. How long would this last?

Frankly, I had just about forgotten about the little, frail drug-addicted woman who had changed my life in unexpected, and what my mother would say were "accidental," ways. And I hadn't laid eyes on the poor, unfortunate husband since that day at his estate. But, as the days passed, I was nagged in the back of my mind about how the white hospital woman, the pitiful drug-addicted woman, had come to possess the sacred objects in the first place. Nothing seemed quite as useless in this whole astonishing event as accepting the history of a past epoch represented by artifacts as just accidental. Perhaps I would end up accepting that, but for the moment, I felt somehow like a needy and uncertain game player.

It was four-thirty in the afternoon when we all trooped over to the meeting place together, the nurses, the aides, the nuns, and even a couple of the doctors. We were gathered again to answer the relentless questions about the death of the wealthy woman, this time questions posed by some kind of Catholic hospital board. It seemed odd that the endless inquiry into this death was apparently never going to stop, yet the death of Allie Eagle hadn't been mentioned for months. Maybe Robert was right about getting a lawyer.

All of the sisters were there from the hospital, their heavy white uniforms sweeping them along like waves on an inviolate sea, their pink faces round like peaches, ripe and innocent at the same time. Bustling, hurrying. Sister Amabolis, wearing her huge black shoes, seemed older today as she lumbered, her lips moving either in prayer or in some kind of mindless fidgeting, across the lawn and the parking lot.

Many others I didn't know had come, too—I guessed from the prefecture or the diocese or from wherever these important church folks hide out when they aren't doing their day jobs. They were looking stern, dressed in solemn black, ready to become part of the tribunal organized as legal authority to administer justice. Waiting in judgment was nothing new to these folks.

I was surprised by this whole thing because I had thought it was all in the past. I hadn't wanted to see the husband again ever in my lifetime, and certainly I hadn't wanted to see him under these circumstances, but I felt almost like an old friend as I watched him from the doorway.

He was seated at the front of the room like he was going to the gallows, and he was pale as a ghost. He looked like he had lost forty pounds. As far as I knew, he was never a heavy man even in times less challenging than these, so it was weight he could ill afford to lose and it made him look emaciated and unwell. His hair, ordinarily thick and glossy and dark, was thinner and dull, and though he always seemed to me to be a handsome man, he no longer looked like a figure of status and wealth. He looked shabby, almost, but as I walked to my seat I could smell his cologne, so I knew he had tried to pull himself together for the occasion.

"We have been asked by the children of the deceased to put forth this inquiry," began the young, black-robed priest, giving us a sort of benign introduction to the fact that the children of the deceased woman were suing the hell out of the hospital and everyone connected with the death. The priest looked important—but, then, to me as a child of mission school they all look important. Maybe he was a bishop or a cardinal even. Maybe not. He wasn't wearing a red cap. Maybe he was consigliere to the order of nuns, the Dominicans, who my classmates at boarding school had dubbed "the meanest people on the face of the earth," and if that were the case, I couldn't expect things to get better for the husband anytime soon.

"As you can see, under these conditions we have no choice. Even though we may think that there has been nothing charged and the police have ended their inquiry and there is not a shred of evidence that anything criminal has happened, you can see that we have no choice."

I wondered about the bias in the introduction. If an inquiry was to be held, it should at least have the appearance of fairness.

He folded his hands in the pious gesture so familiar to me from my school days, and he intoned:

"*Let us pray. God our father, we pray that you help us in our duties today. Our father, who art in heaven, hallowed be thy name . . .*"

I learned that the children were suing the diocese and the hospital and everyone connected with the death for what was called "wrongful" death, and they were trying to get the evidence together to charge the husband with manslaughter. The "gifted" article was part and parcel of the estate matters.

I was worried that I might be named as some kind of co-conspirator, especially when I looked over at Robert, who sat with a smug look on his face like he wanted to incriminate somebody. But I was just being called as a witness again.

As we entered the room I wanted to sit beside the stricken husband, but I didn't, because then they might say we were in it together. The testimony given by everyone throughout the tedious afternoon offered nothing new, so it seemed as the day wore on to be just a formality that the Church was going through in order to assuage the stepchildren, and from the looks on their faces, it wasn't working. Like many organizations, this one seemed impermeable, and it finally ended without any new findings. I wasn't surprised. My testimony was like all the rest: "Yes. I was there. No, I saw and know nothing."

Stiff from sitting for hours in cramped chairs and subdued from the detachment of most of the afternoon's discussion, we walked slowly, the husband and I, to his car. He seemed unduly quiet, almost unable to converse.

It was evening now, and a slight mist had fallen over the town; the windows of the dark buildings all around us, though lighted, seemed dim and distanced. To the left of the parking lot people drifted into the little neighborhood store run by the only dark immigrants in this town, Greeks—with what people thought were strange, unpronounceable names—the only concession to diversity this town had ever made. It was mostly a little candy store, but they had now started serving the steamed coffee made famous by Starbucks.

"I don't know how much more of this I can take," the husband began.

"Why don't you just give them the money?"

"The money?"

"Or whatever it is they want . . ."

"Oh, Big Pipe," he said in a voice both sarcastic and mournful. "This, my friend, isn't about money!"

"It's not?"

"No."

"What's it about then?"

"It's about hate. Selfishness. Years and years of rancor and grievance and loathing. It's about a bunch of wretched people called a 'family' so warped, so mean-spirited for so many years and so many generations that there is no hope."

He shook his head in a despairing gesture and his face was wet. "It is about . . . about . . . evil."

"Evil?!"

"Evil," he repeated. "Something depraved and . . . and . . . wicked."

He struggled for words.

"And I'll never be free of it!"

"What . . . I mean . . . why do you say that? What has happened?"

"It started, I think, with my wife and her father and her grandfather. And it started, I've come to believe, with the bundle, the shirt we've now given back to you.

"And, I think my wife knew about it all along and I think that is why she wanted you to have it. You know, the first time she saw you at the hospital, she told me that you had come there for some reason."

It was beginning to feel creepy, but he went on as though driven by memory.

"In her clear, intelligible moments, she said you were destined, certain, appointed. By the stars. Or something. She didn't know how to explain it, but she said you were there for some reason."

Was this a man going over the edge?

"'Que sera sera,' she would say," and he smiled. "You remember that Doris Day song?"

I didn't.

"She loved that song." For a moment he was lost in the music.

"So, you see," he said in a softened voice, incoherent now, his eyes glittering, "the way they got it was to dig up the graves."

"I thought you said you didn't know how they got it."

"I know I said that. But I know. I know."

Then, back from memory lane, he was all business. "I know how they got it. And so do you!"

He looked at me with red eyes so filled with grief I didn't know what to say, what to do.

"Don't you see? It was wrong! Morally wrong. Ethically wrong. It was wrong in every sense of the word and it was based on the killing of a people, an entire people! They were trying to kill all of you. Don't you understand?"

I could hardly speak.

"Sure. Sure. I understand that. Read a little history and you get that! I guess I've always known that, but your poor wife . . . and her kids—?"

He interrupted: "And that beautiful and sacred thing," he said, on memory lane again, holding out his hands like he was cradling a baby, "that sacred thing of war and death and life, made and worn by your relatives for reasons I will never comprehend, has been in our household against its will . . . *against its will.*"

He grimaced and hunched up his shoulders as though in pain.

"And in the library and in our rooms and in our lives and in our 'collections' of what we considered valuable things for generations, and now . . . now . . . the family of those who stole it has become unhealthy, tortured, deeply troubled . . . because . . . because . . ."

He shuddered.

"We are being punished." His agonized whisper resounded in the dusk.

I was spooked. I wondered if this guy had been reading too much Stephen King.

"Yeah, yeah, I see," I said, feeling that I was on the verge of babbling like he was. "Sure . . . grave robbing is wrong."

But was he saying that such a thing as this crime could infect an entire family? Could it go on for generations? Could it be the cause of the destruction of a woman, a wife and a mother, and the destruction of her family?

"Really," I began, trying to make sense of what he was saying and what it was we didn't know, "the people in her family were not the only people who desecrated Indian graves."

"Yes-s-s," he said, and he grabbed my arms, excited that I was beginning to get it, as though I had never heard of all of this and now that he was explaining I was being enlightened—like I was just now beginning to get it.

"Yes . . . you are right . . . hundreds of white people did that; thousands, maybe—hundreds of thousands, maybe. The bones of Indians, the sacred stuff from the graves, these things are everywhere in museums, libraries, repositories, and private collections, hospitals and institutions all over this country! And even in Europe. All kinds of stuff!!"

He stopped to take a deep breath.

"And so," I asked, "are they all to be tortured? Are they all to live sordid lives and contaminated lives? And does it go on generation after generation?"

He wasn't listening to me, but instantly I liked the question. Even asking the question out loud gave me a moment of clarity and I thought, why not? *Yes . . . why not? Of course, there are no accidents . . . maybe there is no fate and no destiny, even though the old-young woman wanted to think so and the husband now was spouting this nonsense . . . The surety of Dorothy's explanation was making sense . . . maybe it has something to do with evil . . . evil is a real thing, of course . . . Whatever the case, some people survive and others don't and nobody is blameless, and at the same time there is no one to blame and there is no great pretension and, yet, we all have to pay the price of our past and take on the crimes of our ancestors.*

As quickly as I thought of all this, the thoughts were gone and it just seemed like a terrible contradiction . . . This guy was getting to me. Was I getting nutty, too?

He went on, still moaning and groaning about his grief.

"I didn't know any of this," he was saying, paying no attention to me, as though I wasn't standing there with my mouth open. "I didn't know any of this, about the shirt or about the grave robbing, when I married her. I was her third husband, you know, and she was already sick, even then. I only knew that she came from an important family, that they had lots of money. We, she and I, didn't have the artifacts until after the death of her father. Then they came to us from his estate."

His fingers combed his sweaty hair. He leaned against the car and crossed his skinny legs and took another deep breath.

"But that's not why I married her. She was a beautiful woman. And kind. And good."

I said nothing.

"I know you couldn't see that in her. By the time you knew her it had taken its toll and she was gone; the beautiful woman who was my wife, my life, was gone."

He buried his face in his hands.

"God. I miss her. How I have missed her for years! She's been gone a long time, you know."

He was going to get maudlin on me, and I was wanting to leave, but I didn't want to leave without saying something. Something. Anything. Why did I continue to be distressed by this man's pain? The insidious questions about how all of this mattered to me seemed nothing if not just plain curious.

I usually don't waste time on matters that have no real consequence, but there was something . . . something about this man's simple, incorruptible goodness. For several long moments I couldn't think of anything to say, and in the silence of that pause, he mused: "The question is, Philip, what happens to people? What happens . . . when . . ."

He, too, seemed at a loss.

"Umm . . ." I muttered, trying to seize on this moment of familiarity, to find something we could agree on and something that would make things better for him, at least momentarily. "Well, you are right to ask that question . . . what happens . . . well . . ."

Apparently, I didn't know what the question was, either.

"What happens is . . . you've done the right thing. It wasn't you and it wasn't your wife who stole things. And now these sacred things are returned and all is well. You and your wife are good people. Good people can't be punished for what bad people do, can they?"

He looked at me for a long time and then, in a voice filled with suffering, said, "Pipe, you are so naive!"

I stared.

Now he was going to insult me, huh? It is an insult to an Indian to be called "naive" about the scope of the white man's history. Especially an Indian raised by the old man and Auntie Aurelia. Lifting my eyebrows I decided it would be best if I ignored this comment. For his sake, if not mine. It wasn't naiveté on my part. And the idea that he would think me gullible and simple-minded told me that I was successful at hiding any truthful thinking about this whole situation. My duplicity had paid off, at least for now. I'd learned how to do it and felt pleased with myself.

My motive then was just to get through these awful moments. Maybe I'd just let it go, but if a person like myself could listen for years and years to the Christian rhetoric spouted in boarding schools on an Indian reservation and stay naive, let me say *that* would be a miracle! And, for me, the age of miracles is past.

It's incredible that this man thinks I am unsuspecting . . . and gullible, I thought. I let it go, though, because this good and gentle man couldn't be expected to know that since very early days, my mode of dealing with a foolish world has been cynicism, not naiveté. Perception is half the function of reality, so what does it matter that I didn't believe the bullshit that I was spouting, that *good people can't be punished for what bad people do*, any more than he did.

Let it go, I thought.

No one knew more than I that the history of a genocidal racism which was at the core of this transaction was unforgivable, and that people who have always been the benefactors of its criminality are never to be forgiven. Never. Not redeemed, either.

Should I have put all of this into some kind of biblical terms that he might understand and say what I really thought . . . that he was unredeemable? That his awful wife was, too? Did he really want me to say that? What did he expect from me? Was his need to call me naive just another negotiation? If so, I wasn't going to go for it. Maybe in retrospect I should have. But what happens, happens, and a person should not live in regret because of mistakes or miscalculations.

At this point the guy was wringing his hands, and if there is anything I can't stand more than making history a foolish thing, it's hand-wringing. First of all, it doesn't get you anywhere, and secondly, it delays the inevitable.

What it did at that moment was make me forget about what could happen and who was at risk. In the same way that I had not been forewarned those days so many months ago when Uncle Tony offed himself, I was again unable to give some thought to the awful reactions to years of grief and anguish that happen when personal needs take over.

Not admitting that grief often ends in the ubiquitous human curse called hatred, and that it would intervene again before this day ended, I mistakenly thought we had time. I've always thought time was on our side as human beings, but now I've learned otherwise.

I leaned forward and, just for the hell of it, just because I was there and just because he was so needy and just because I thought we had time, I struggled for something to say to avoid any further emotional outburst from him.

As I did so, and just before the words came, I saw a movement out of the corner of my eye. Out of the darkness a man dressed in loose-fitting clothing, a figure of monstrous, angry energy, was reaching up into the sky, to bring down a shining knife into the heart of the grieving man, and I heard the shouts of those around me and felt Robert shove me aside as he rushed to administer to the dying man.

People came out of nowhere and fell upon the weeping and cursing stepson and wrestled him to the ground amid much shouting and screaming.

I was pushed down in the oncoming rush of several onlookers who, unafraid, either wanted to help or get closer to the action.

I glanced up and saw the mute Catholic sisters silently standing all in a row, mouths open but no sound coming out, like a tragic chorus in some great dumb play, some of them dressed in white and others in black, horror written on their provincial faces—actors whose parts were confirmed as the hired attendants at a funeral.

The huge knife slid from the perpetrator's white hands onto the pavement. Lights suddenly were everywhere and the whole night sky exploded in color.

I crawled to where the husband's body was gushing blood from what seemed like every artery, and his suit jacket and tie and shirt were drenched in red blood, and he turned to me and said, "I will see . . ." But he could not finish his sentence.

His hair was plastered to his forehead and blood was oozing from his pale lips, and as I watched, his breath stopped.

CHAPTER 15

I t was done. It was over.

And at first I thought I felt nothing but relief as I stood up, disengaged myself from the crowd that had gathered, and walked slowly across the shriveled gray lawn to the Limo.

The feeling that the husband was an old friend seemed to disappear like scent in the wind, and I thought he was nothing more than a man who had held illegal trust over a sacred object, and now it was done and any relationship that we may have had was depleted, and any agreement that might have been made was left months ago at the graveside with my relatives who had put the sacred shirt to rest.

One can do nothing in the face of such stunning pain, I thought. I no longer asked the question of whether this was history or just a series of "accidents"; if it was destiny; or if it had any deeper meaning than the absurdity of being human.

Nothing is paid and nothing is owed, I told myself under my breath—an amazing deal for those of us who might have been forced against our wills into investing something into this miserable world. An amazing deal for those who will not believe in accidents.

I looked back at the scene, now clogged with shouting, agitated people, and saw a lifeless figure crumpled in a heap, growing cold with every passing moment, a man who until the last days of his life had never understood his role in a serious offense against humanity deeply shrouded in an awful history for which no one gets to blame anyone else.

I sat silently in the Limo and felt my eyes get red and moist. It wasn't his fault, I said over and over again. It wasn't his fault. Nor was it mine.

I sat behind the wheel. In a moment I saw another black and white police car careen up the street and skid to a stop, the cop on his radio calling for an ambulance, his lights blinking into the darkness. Then I drove slowly through the narrow streets and wondered about towns like this one where I have come to live however briefly, however accidentally.

Who are the people sleeping in these dark houses along this silent street? Where do they go and what do they do when the sun leaves and the lights are dimmed?

Are they lying in their comfortable beds reading by lamplight, or are they shouting at one another in after-dark anger and frustration from days of dissatisfaction?

Do they know us? What are they keeping that does not belong to them? Who will their children be?

I drove slowly, listening only to the ominous and depressing sounds of the worn-out springs of the Limo at every turn and at every stoplight and every time I stepped on the brakes. I couldn't turn on the radio or the Crown Butte tapes, and I couldn't cry. At that moment, there were no thoughts of the future to comfort me. My feeling of sorrow even extended to the recent death of Kevin . . . missing his skinny, dark presence. Where was he when you needed him? I always made excuses for him and now I felt that he left me high and dry. He would not haunt me deliberately, but I had learned from him to listen to the signs around me . . . and from Tony. Surely, the memory of how the both of them looked at every new day with some kind of laughable goodwill would protect me. I knew if they were here to witness the cynical mishaps of my accidental life, I didn't need to try to be worthy of anything. Not now. Not even later.

I didn't want to be seen by anyone in this distressed state, so I shifted down and drove even slower. Just then, I noticed with alarm some movement in front of me. The dim lights shone on the white line in the middle of the street, suddenly wavering, revealing a snakelike, twisting and winding fog. Staring at it, I noticed a sinuous, soundless, irresistible form that I could hardly see. My eyes stung and

I was filled with amazement as the soft, limbless form in front of me seemed to dip and run and pause like a dancing supernatural being.

It lasted only a moment, but I knew as I stared that I would visit a place I had only heard about, a place untouched by reality.

What I was seeing in front of me was a reminder that mere mortals are not in charge of everything. The wavering thing, which disappeared in a moment, reminded me that there is a place up north where a snake edifice made by the people exists alongside all the other powers of the world, and I knew then that I would go there:

Keyapi (they say this)

There are nearly a thousand stones, including two for the eyes of the serpent; they are the size of an egg. And the head is ten feet long. Even the dam building all up and down the Missouri has not obliterated this structure, which means that it simply speaks to the constancy of human and earthly possibilities.

I stared into the road for a long time, feeling obscure, unknown, desolate. This important religious site now given its own logic made me slowly aware, while there alone, that its own powerful shape didn't need to dominate the beautiful view of the river and the prairie landscape where the wolves and other creatures live, that it could simply overlook the vistas below and echo the forms of the earth without lending itself to any kind of literal explanation.

Any man who believes in the power of ancient rock shrines, I knew then, could simply fade into the landscape.

It might be said that the Indians told no one where the ancient mystery was located, neither did they say what it meant, so most people eventually forgot where it was and why they made it and why it was important. All we have known in our lives is that they made art of events and ideas important to them as they were the ever-present and traditional occupants of the plains, going about their days tracking the sun and remembering the earth.

In the night a silent snow fell unexpectedly, and I was unconscious of its gentle falling. It covered everything in sight in the few hours of darkness as I drove to my place.

Catching sight of the fading stars, I imagined the snake stretching out over the land, the snow covering its body and its eyes covered over, too, with winter, the wolves sniffing nearby. The Old Grandfather is coming without warning, I thought as I looked out of the window, watching the falling snow obscure the moon and drench everything in white.

This is no accident, I mused. I couldn't help but smile.

The Old Ones would stay as long as they liked, and I was coming to the slow realization that there would be dancing here eventually on these empty roads I've been "accidentally" traveling.

I knew at that moment that once in a while, perhaps sometime in the not-so-distant future, I might be privileged to catch sight of the dancing. It might happen in the spring. I'll wait. I'm good at waiting.

As I squinted at the light out across the city, I knew I wanted to see the stones stretching out over the land, the open tall grass prairie, the important serpent mound made of ancient boulders. I drove on and parked the Limo and rested for just a moment, and then, gathering what energy I had left, headed into the house. I heard my footsteps fall heavily on the shaky porch steps. I opened the squeaky, unlocked door. I let myself in and went directly to my room and lay down without undressing.

I lay there for hours without moving, my eyes wide open. I struggled with the sleeplessness of someone who has been in the thick of things for too long and now is burdened with the awful feeling of having too many memories. I wished Kevin could go to the open prairie with me. I longed to see Dorothy again.

.　　■　　■

The next day, feeling like I had only imagined the road scene for reasons no one could say, I knew it was time to seek a new road. I silently congratulated myself as I went into the hallway and with great confidence telephoned the sister superior to ask her to cut through the red tape and somehow get them to award me a scholarship to Mount Marty College. Yeah, Kev, going far might be possible.

While the kindly old nun agreed and with great enthusiasm gushed about my great and potential future, my confidence waned, and momentarily I felt a little sheepish, like a smooth or slick or a too-cool phony. It has always been my view that there have never been many great options for me, then or now. This seemed to be the best I could do, leave this sleeping neighborhood that would never wake up. I had to take my chances.

Later, Clarissa asks: "You're leaving again?"

A cautious man, I don't answer. I go to my room and begin to pack and let her sit at the window to watch, admitting to myself that she would probably show up in my life every now and then like the proverbial bad penny. No more indignation, no more contempt. I hand her the tape player and the sponge mop, useful things for her to keep. The hairbrush I lift carefully and pack it next to the socks.

Outside, the grass is starved for rain in spite of the light skiff of snow.

"I'm heading north for now," I tell my mother.

Later, sunglasses perched on my nose, I am speeding down Matthews Street in the Limo, the Crown Butte singers blasting, making it my business to find that dancing road . . . through history and difficult times . . . toward the shapes that are open to the sky, a cure for my own exile.